FROM WATSON'S SCRAPBOOK

My dear friend Sherlock Holmes was so pleased with the previous issue, which was entirely devoted to him, that he is now a bit despondent, inasmuch as he will need to wait till the twentieth number before it happens again.

It also took some doing to let me reprint the "Norwood" adventure; it was, after all, one of his less successful efforts. He finally agreed, though he suggested that I do not allow this issue to lay about in our rooms for him to see. Ah, well…

In the ensuing pages, the estimable Mr Grochot has rendered my notes into an excellent and accurate recounting of the Addleton tragedy.

And now here is my colleague Mr Kaye…

—John H Watson, M D

I am pleased to offer three articles in this, the sixteenth edition of *Sherlock Holmes Mystery Magazine*. Peter James Quirk, whom I had the pleasure of meeting at the New York branch of the MWA (Mystery Writers of America), reviews the evidence for and against the British monarch Richard III as to whether he killed the two princes, or whether someone else entirely was responsible. In this, of course, the great Josephine Tey did a fine job of defending Richard in her unusual mystery novel, *The Daughter of Time*. I never knew what her title meant until I mentioned it to my late friend José Ferrer, who explained that there is a saying that "Truth is the daughter of time."

Dan Di Quinzio devotes himself to a history of W. S. Baring-Gould, who gave Holmesian devotees the "official" biography of the Great Detective, the Annotated edition of the sixty cases, as well as a biography of the sleuth rumored to be Holmes's son, Nero Wolfe of West 35th Street, Manhattan.

Gary Lovisi tells of the fascinating correspondence between Dr. Watson's literary agent Arthur Conan Doyle and Robert Louis Stevenson.

The other stories in this issue include one author new to these pages: John Grant. The other five have appeared here before—Dianne Neral El, Steve Liskow, Laird Long, Richard Lupoff, and Stan Trybulski.

The coming issue of SHMM will feature a new tale by the estimable Kim Newman as well as more stories by Laird Long and Steve Liskow. Our regular cartoonist Marc Bilgrey also will have a new adventure for us.

There will also be two remarkable articles about criminals, one of whom was friends to nearly all of the Brooklyn police force, while the other became one of England's most important spies during World War II.

Till then, do write to Mrs Hudson—and remember that we are always interested in new articles, as well as fiction.

Canonically Yours,
—Marvin Kaye

SHERLOCK HOLMES
MYSTERY MAGAZINE

VOL. 6, NO. 1   Issue #16

"MRS. HUDSON WOULD LIKE TO MAKE A REQUEST."

MARC BILGREY

Publisher: John Betancourt
Editor: Marvin Kaye
Non-fiction Editor: Carla Coupe
Assistant Editor: Steve Coupe

Sherlock Holmes Mystery Magazine is published by Wildside Press, LLC. Single copies: $10.00 + $3.00 postage. U.S. subscriptions: $59.95 (postage paid) for the next 6 issues in the U.S.A., from: Wildside Press LLC, Subscription Dept. 9710 Traville Gateway Dr., #234; Rockville MD 20850. International subscriptions: see our web site at www.wildsidemagazines.com. Available as an ebook through all major ebook etailers, or our web site, www.wildsidemagazines.com.

COMING NEXT TIME...

STORIES! ARTICLES!
SHERLOCK HOLMES & DR. WATSON!

Sherlock Holmes Mystery Magazine #17
is just a few months away...watch for it!

Not a subscriber yet?
Send $59.95 for 6 issues (postage paid in the U.S.) to:

Wildside Press LLC
Attn: Subscription Dept.
9710 Traville Gateway Dr. #234
Rockville MD 20850

You can also subscribe online at
www.wildsidemagazines.com

THE IRONIC STORY OF THE STEVENSON - DOYLE LETTERS

by Gary Lovisi

Synchronicity in discovery can be a wonderful thing. When I came upon a two-volume set of *The Letters of Robert Louis Stevenson* I had no idea what gold I would discover within the 900+ pages—some of it, my dear friends, of a Sherlockian nature!

It is not a story of horror, such as that written by Stevenson in his classic, *Dr. Jekyll & Mr. Hyde*, but a tale that contains fascinating irony. In fact, it is a strange and interesting story, yet strikes a sad note about the wonderful relationship between two of the most famous and beloved writers of all time. Two men whose works still live with us today and have stood the test of time.

Letter writing was once the major communication medium back in the day. When famed author (and creator of *Treasure Island* [1883] and *Dr. Jekyll & Mr. Hyde* [1887] among many others), Robert Louis Stevenson wrote the first of four letters to Arthur Conan Doyle in 1893, it was because Stevenson greatly admired Doyle and his work. That feeling of admiration was very much reciprocated by Sir Arthur. Doyle admired Stevenson's *Treasure Island* and considered *Dr. Jekyll & Mr. Hyde* a masterpiece of Gothic storytelling.

Stevenson's four letters to Doyle appear in a rare two-volume edition *The Letters of Robert Louis Stevenson* edited by Sidney Colvin (Charles Scribners Sons, 1901, New York), the first US edition of Stevenson's letters. These attractive books are in red cloth binding with gold lettering on cover, spine and top pages edges. Volume One features letters to Stevenson's friends and family from his younger days from 1868 to 1885. However, we are concerned with Volume Two, containing letters from 1886 to 1894, written to such luminaries as Rudyard Kipling, Henry James, J.M. Barrie, William Morris, Andrew Lang—and his four letters to Arthur Conan Doyle. While the two volumes contain over 900 pages of Stevenson's letters, editor Sidney Colvin (who knew the author well) stated that they formed a mere 15-20 percent of Stevenson's overall letters. Interestingly enough, it seemed Stevenson did not like writing letters very much, and he considered himself a bad correspondent.

In his letters to Doyle, Stevenson writes of his recognition of Dr. Joseph Bell as being the basis for Sherlock Holmes. Ironically, it seems the two authors—both Scotsmen who lived in Edinburgh—actually knew Dr. Bell. Even more ironic, Stevenson graduated from the University of Edinburgh in 1875, a year before Doyle enrolled there to study medicine. But the irony of this tale does not stop there.

Stevenson was a fan of Doyle's Sherlock Holmes stories and even commented on the Holmes story "The Engineer's Thumb" in one letter, and on the influence that Doyle had on his classic novel, *Treasure Island*.

In the book *Arthur Conan Doyle, A Life in Letters*, edited by Jon Lellenberg, Daniel Stashower, and Charles Folly (Penguin Press, 2007), some of Doyle's letters, most to his mother, Mary, are published. On page 430, Doyle mentions the four letters he received from Stevenson, and wrote about them, "I had the most encouraging letters from him in 1893 and 1894. 'O frolic fellow-spookiest' was Stevenson's curious term of personal salutation on one of these, which showed that he shared my interest in psychic research but did not take it very seriously." In fact, I believe Stevenson was lightly teasing Doyle about his spiritualist leanings.

Arthur and Innes on their way to America.

However, as I have stated, there was much more. Stevenson writes about a meeting between the two great authors. This was a rather difficult accomplishment at the time, since in 1893-94—the time Stevenson wrote his four letters to Doyle—he was living far away in the village of Vailima, on the Pacific island of Samoa. Doyle was living in the UK. Almost ten thousand miles separated the two men. However, by this time Stevenson and Doyle had become famous authors and also world travelers—so that while such a meeting might be time-consuming or difficult to schedule—it was eminently possible. The two men very much wanted to meet and the logistics of such a meeting were mentioned in Stevenson's letters.

In fact, Conan Doyle made definite plans to extend his September, 1894 American Tour. The plan was to leave from San Francisco and include a visit to Stevenson in Samoa—where RLS had made his permanent home since 1890.

Stevenson's correspondence to Doyle is fascinating and quite lively, at times whimsical and even poetic. The irony and sadness is what we know so many years later, which does not come through in the letters, though Stevenson in his last letter to Doyle does mention his own death.

THE HOUSE AT VAILIMA AFTER THE ADDITIONS.

Now, in his own words, here are Stevenson's four letters to Doyle, and one reply from Doyle that I was able to find. Here is the actual text of the letters:

Letter: to Doyle

VAILIMA, APIA, SAMOA, APRIL 5TH, 1893

DEAR SIR, – You have taken many occasions to make yourself very agreeable to me, for which I might in decency have thanked you earlier. It is now my turn; and I hope you will allow me to offer you my compliments on your very ingenious and very interesting adventures of Sherlock Holmes. That is the class of literature that I like when I have the toothache. As a matter of fact, it was a pleurisy I was enjoying when I took the volume up; and it will interest you as a medical man to know that the cure was for the moment effectual. Only the one thing troubles me: can this be my old friend Joe Bell? – I am, yours very truly,

ROBERT LOUIS STEVENSON

P.S. – And lo, here is your address supplied me here in Samoa! But do not take mine, O frolic fellow Spookist, from the same source; mine is wrong.

R.L.S.

Letter: Response from Doyle to Stevenson's April 5, 1893 letter

I'm so glad Sherlock Holmes helped to pass an hour for you. He's a bastard between Joe Bell [a famous Edinburgh surgeon] and Poe's Monsieur Dupin (much diluted). I trust that I may never write a word about him again. I had rather that you knew me by my *White Company*. I'm sending it on the chance that you have not seen it.

Letter: To Doyle

VAILIMA, JULY 12, 1893

MY DEAR DR. CONAN DOYLE – THE WHITE COMPANY has not yet turned up; but when it does—which I suppose will be in the next mail—you shall hear news of me. I have a great talent for compliment, accompanied by a hateful, even a diabolic frankness.

Delighted to hear I have a chance of seeing you and Mrs. Doyle; Mrs. Stevenson bids me say (what is too true) that our rations are often spare. Are you Great Eaters? Please reply. As to ways and means, here is what you will have to do. Leave San Francisco by the down mail, get off at Samoa, and twelve days or a fortnight later, you can continue your journey to Auckland per Upolu, which will give you a look at Tonga and possibly Fiji by the way. Make this a FIRST PART OF YOUR PLANS. A fortnight, even of Vailima diet, could kill nobody.

We are in the midst of war here; rather a nasty business, with the head-taking; and there seem signs of other trouble. But I believe you need make no change in your design to visit us. All should be well over; and if it were not, why! You need not leave the steamer – Yours very truly,

ROBERT LOUIS STEVENSON

Letter: To Doyle

VAILIMA, AUGUST 23RD, 1893

MY DEAR DR. CONAN DOYLE, – I am reposing after a somewhat severe experience upon which I think it my duty to report to you. Immediately after dinner this evening it occurred to me to re-narrate to my native overseer Simele your story of THE ENGINEER'S THUMB. And, sir, I have done it. It was necessary, I need hardly say, to go somewhat farther afield than you have done. To explain (for instance) what a railway is, what a steam hammer, what a coach and horse, what coining, what a criminal, and what the police. I pass over other and no less necessary explanations. But I did actually succeed; and if you could have seen the drawn, anxious features and the bright, feverish eyes of Simele, you would have (for the moment at least) tasted glory. You might perhaps think that, were you to come to Samoa, you might be introduced as the Author of THE ENGINEER'S THUMB. Disabuse yourself. They do not know what it is to make up a story. THE ENGINEER'S THUMB (God forgive me) was narrated as a piece of actual and factual history. Nay, and more, I who write to you have had the indiscretion to perpetrate a trifling piece of fiction entitled THE BOTTLE IMP. Parties who come up to visit my unpretentious mansion, after having admired the ceilings by Vanderputty and the tapestry by Gobbling, manifest towards the end a certain uneasiness which proves them to be fellows of an infinite delicacy. They may be seen to shrug a brown shoulder, to roll up a speaking eye, and at last secret burst from them: 'Where is the bottle?' Alas, my friends (I feel tempted to say), you will find it by the Engineer's Thumb! Talofa-soifuia.

Oa'u, O lau no moni, O Tusitala.

More commonly known as,

R.L. STEVENSON.

Have read the REFUGEES; Conde and old P. Murat very good; Louis XIV and Louvois with the letter bag very rich. You have reached a trifle wise perhaps; too MANY celebrities? Though I was delighted to re-encounter my old friend Du Chaylu. Old Murat is perhaps your high water mark; 'tis excellently human, cheerful and real. Do it again. Madame de Maintenon struck me as quite good. Have you any document for the decapitation? It sounds steepish.

The devil of all that first part is that you see old Dumas; yet your Louis XIV is DISTINCTLY GOOD. I am much interested with this book, which fulfills a good deal, and promises more. Question: How far a Historical Novel should be wholly episodic? I incline to that view, with trembling. I shake hands with you on old Murat.

R.L.S.

Letter: To Doyle

[This letter refers to articles by various authors in the magazine, *Idler,* under the title "My First Book."]

VAILIMA, SAMOA, SEPTEMBER 9, 1894

MY DEAR CONAN DOYLE, – If you found anything to entertain you in my TREASURE ISLAND article, it may amuse you to know that you owe it entirely to yourself. YOUR 'First Book' was by some accident read aloud one night in my Baronial 'All. I was consumedly amused by it, so was the whole family, and we proceeded to hunt up back IDLERS and read the whole series. It is a rattling good series, even people whom you would not expect came in quite the proper tone—Miss Braddon, for instance, who was really one of the best where all are good—or all but one! …in short, I fell in love with 'The First Book' series, and determined that it should be all our first books, and that I could not hold back where the white plume of Conan Doyle waved gallantly in the front. I hope they will republish them, though it's a grievous thought to me that that effigy in the German cap—likewise the other effigy of the noisome old man with the long hair, telling indelicate stories to a couple of deformed negresses in a rancid shanty full of wreckage—should be perpetuated. I may seem to speak in pleasantry—it is only a seeming—that German cap, sir, would be found, when I come to die, imprinted on my heart. Enough—my heart is too full. Adieu. – Yours very truly,

ROBERT LOUIS STEVENSON

✗   ✗   ✗   ✗

Alas, with plans set and both men willing, the greatest irony of all is that these two giants of popular fiction would never meet. The most ironic event of all—obviously instituted by the Fates themselves—in the same month that Conan Doyle killed off Sherlock

Holmes at the Reichenbach Falls—Robert Louis Stevenson suffered a brain hemorrhage and died in his beloved Samoa. He was only 44 years old.

"THE PLAZA" (PORTSMOUTH SQUARE).

THE FAVOURITE LOUNGING-PLACE OF ROBERT LOUIS STEVENSON IN SAN FRANCISCO,
WITH THE MEMORIAL TO HIM DESIGNED BY BRUCE PORTER AND WILLIS POLK.

References:

The Letters of Robert Louis Stevenson Volumes 1 and 2, edited by Sidney Colvin, Charles Scribners Sons, 1901, New York. Stevenson photos are reproduced from these editions.

Arthur Conan Doyle, A Life in Letters edited by Jon Lellenberg, Daniel Stashower, and Charles Foley, Penguin Press, 2007.

"Dr. Doyle and Mr. Stevenson" by Mark Shanahan, Alley Theater website.

"Robert Louis Stevenson's Letters to Doyle 1893-4" in *Mark-ings*, internet, no author listed, June 21, 2012.

Gary Lovisi is an MWA Edgar-nominated author for Best Short Story for his Sherlock Holmes pastiche "The Adventure of The Missing Detective." He is a Holmes fan, collector, and writes various articles and short stories of, and about, The Great Detective, some of which have appeared in this magazine. He is the editor of *Paperback Parade* and *Hardboiled* magazines, and of the recent Sherlock Holmes anthology, *The Great Detective: His Further Adventures* (Wildside Press). You can find out more about him and his work at his website: www.gryphonbooks.com.

THE CONTRIBUTIONS OF WILLIAM S. BARING-GOULD TO MODERN SHERLOCKIAN SCHOLARSHIP

by Daniel DiQuinzio

The writer William Stuart Baring-Gould was born in Minnesota in 1913. He was the grandson of the Victorian writer Sabine Baring-Gould, who wrote both novels and ghost stories. Sabine Baring-Gould also authored the sixteen-volume series *The Lives of the Saints* between 1872 and 1877. Although his grandfather died in 1924, William S. Baring-Gould inherited his grandfather's passion for literature.

After high school graduation, Baring-Gould attended the University of Minnesota where he studied marketing. There he met Lucile Marguerite Woody, whom he married in 1936. After graduation, the marketing department of Hearst Publications employed him. In 1938, he left Hearst Publications for Time, Inc., for which he worked as the copy editor for several magazines while also contributing literary work to some of these periodicals. He became the creative director of Time, Inc.'s circulation department.

In 1957, he published the book *The Lure of Limerick*. In 1962, he coedited *The Annotated Mother Goose* with his wife. However, Baring-Gould's true passion was the world of Sherlock Holmes. In 1948, he published the essay, "A New Chronology of Holmes and Doctor Watson," which was his first piece of Sherlockian scholarship. The *Baker Street Journal* serialized this essay in the fall and spring issues of 1948. In 1952, he was invested in the Baker Street Irregulars under the name "The Gloria Scott."

In 1955, Baring-Gould authored the book *The Chronological Holmes,* which was an expansion of his 1948 essay. It was printed and discussed among the members of the Baker Street Irregulars.

Baring-Gould later utilized this text as a reference guide while writing the two volumes that comprise *The Annotated Sherlock Holmes*, in which he organized the Sherlock Holmes stories by his own, sometimes disputed, chronological order.

However, *The Annotated Sherlock Holmes* was not Baring-Gould's masterpiece. Instead, that honor belongs to his earlier work, *Sherlock Holmes of Baker Street: A Life of The World's First Consulting Detective*, which was published in 1962. This book treated Sherlock Holmes as though he were an historical figure. As such, the book chronicles the life of Sherlock Holmes until his death, which Baring-Gould theorized occurred in 1957.

This technique blends the original text of the stories with new material. As a result, the narration of the novel switches between first person and third person. Within *Sherlock Holmes of Baker Street: A Life of the World's First Consulting Detective*, Baring-Gould proposed several theories about both "the Canon" of Sherlock Holmes, as well as its chronology.

Although Baring-Gould published multiple Sherlockian articles during his life, he specialized as a chronologist. However, he was not the first Sherlockian to construct a chronology of the Sherlock Holmes stories. That honor belonged to the Reverend Ronald Knox, who in 1911 published the essay *Studies in the Literature of Sherlock Holmes*, which included a brief chronological outline of "the Canon" of the two collections of Holmes stories along with the published novels. The "Canon" was incomplete, therefore Reverend Knox's chronology was also incomplete.

The first complete chronology was Harold Wilmerding Bell's book *Sherlock Holmes and Dr. Watson: The Chronology of their Adventures*, which was published in 1934. Another chronology of Holmes and Watson was Theodore S. Blankley's book *Sherlock Holmes: Fact or Fiction*, published that same year.

Baring-Gould divided the Holmes stories into different periods as though they were Socratic dialogues based on their chronological date. He created seven chronological periods. The first was the early years of Sherlock Holmes. This period contained the stories "The *Gloria Scott*," which occurred while Holmes was a university student, and "The Musgrave Ritual," which occurred after Holmes left the university. These stories also occurred before Holmes first met Dr. John H. Watson in 1881.

The next period covered the early years of the partnership between Holmes and Watson. It began with the first novel, A *Study in Scarlet*, which occurs in 1881. It lasted until 1886. The next period spanned from 1886 to 1891. It ended with the final battle between Sherlock Holmes and Professor Moriarty. The fourth chronological period began in 1894 with the return of Sherlock Holmes to London and lasted until the year 1902.

The three remaining chronological periods covered the final years of the partnership between Holmes and Watson. According to Baring-Gould, the year 1903 contained the stories "The Adventure of the Three Gables" and "The Adventure of the Creeping Man." It also contained the stories "The Adventure of the Blanched Soldier," before which Watson had "deserted me for a wife, the only selfish act which I can recall in our association," and "The Adventure of the Mazarin Stone."

The remaining two cases occurred after Sherlock Holmes abandoned his practice in 1907 and entered retirement in the Sussex Downs. In 1909, Holmes dealt with the mysterious death of Fitzroy McPherson, the science master "at Harold Stackhurst's well-known coaching establishment" near the Sussex Downs, as chronicled in the story "The Adventure of the Lion's Mane." In 1914, Holmes emerged from retirement to help British intelligence thwart the German spy Von Bork. Watson chronicled this adventure in the short story entitled "His Last Bow."

Within "the Canon," the sole information about the ancestors of Sherlock Holmes is found in the short story "The Greek Interpreter."

"To some extent," he answered thoughtfully, "my ancestors were country squires who appear to have led much the same life as is natural to their class. But none-the-less, my turn that way is in my veins and may have come with my grandmother, who was the sister of Vernet, the French artist."

This would make Holmes the great-grandson of Carle Vernet, who lived from 1758 to 1835. It could also make Holmes the great-grandson of Claude Joseph Vernet, who lived from 1714 to 1789.

Sherlock Holmes of Baker Street: A Life of The World's First Consulting Detective depicts Yorkshire as the ancestral home of the Holmes family. The Holmes estate is located in the area known as North Riding. To this manor house, Baring-Gould gave the name Mycroft.

This depiction builds upon a theory suggested by Rufus S. Tucker in the essay "Genealogical Notes on Holmes." This essay was initially published in 1944. It was later reprinted in the collection *Profile by Gaslight: An Irregular Reader About The Private Life of Sherlock Holmes.*

North Riding is home to manors known as croft. This is an old Saxon term for an enclosed field. This manor was named Mycroft to designate it from the crofts belonging to the neighbors of the Holmes family. Tucker theorized that as the older son, Mycroft "was doomed to bear the name of the family estate." He also theorized that the father of Sherlock Holmes was named either Sigurd or Siger, as Holmes "sometimes signed himself Sigerson, a Norwegian form of Sigurdsson." In addition, he proposed that Holmes's grandfather was named Sherrinford.

Baring-Gould gave the name Siger Holmes to the father of Sherlock Holmes. This man was the Squire of Mycroft. He was a second son, whose brother died in 1844 in "a fall from a horse." As the remaining son, Siger Holmes inherited the Mycroft estate and the surrounding lands. That year he married Violet Sherrinford. She was the daughter of Sir Edward Sherinnford and one of the Vernet sisters.

Neither Holmes nor Watson refers to the existence of Siger Holmes within "the Canon." Baring-Gould resolved this problem by proposing that Holmes angered his father by deciding to become a consulting detective. In response, Squire Holmes banished his son from the family estate. Until the current Squire died, Sherlock Holmes could never "return to the house and lands in Yorkshire."

"The Greek Interpreter" also marks the first appearance of a relative of Sherlock Holmes.

"When I say, therefore, that Mycroft has better powers of observation than I, you may take it that I am speaking the exact and literal truth."

"Is he your junior?"

"No, he is seven years my senior."

Despite being the older brother, Mycroft did not succeed Siger Holmes as the Squire of Mycroft. Instead, his employer is the British government, for which he "audits the books in some of the government departments." Mycroft reappears in the short story, "The Adventure of the Bruce-Partington Plans." In the years between the two stories, within the British government Mycroft has become "the central exchange, the clearinghouse, which makes out the balance." On multiple occasions, Mycroft's word has "decided the national policy."

This prompted Baring-Gould to speculate on the existence of a third Holmes brother who was older than either Sherlock or Mycroft. This brother, Baring-Gould declared, was Sherrinford Holmes. He was named for the children's maternal grandfather, Sir Edward Sherrinford.

Sherrinford Holmes was born in March 1844 in Yorkshire. Many Sherlockian scholars believe that Sherlock Holmes was born in the year 1854. As such, Sherrinford Holmes would be ten years older than Sherlock. As Mycroft Holmes is seven years older than Sherlock, his birth occurred in the year 1847, which makes Sherrinford three years older than Mycroft. According to Baring-Gould, Mycroft was named for Mycroft, the older brother of Squire Siger Holmes.

As the eldest of the Holmes brothers, Sherrinford would "inherit the family holdings in Yorkshire." This freed Mycroft to enter employment with the British government. It also freed Sherlock to become a consulting detective.

In *Sherlock Holmes of Baker Street*, Baring-Gould postulated that the Holmes family engaged in frequent international travel. The family's first sojourn began in 1855, during which they traveled to many European cities. In 1858, the family temporarily settled in Montpellier, where "many of Mrs. Holmes maternal relatives, the Vernets, had moved."

Late in 1858, the family returned to London after the health of Sir Edward Sherrinford declined. He died in the fall of 1858. Afterwards, the family embarked on another international sojourn. This trip lasted until 1860. Upon their return to London, the Holmes children attended boarding schools.

Over the past century, many writers of Holmes pastiches have made frequent use of Professor Moriarty. However, he only appeared in the short story "The Final Problem," which was published in 1893. Moriarty is also mentioned in the final Holmes novel, *The Valley of Fear*.

"The Final Problem" describes Moriarty as being a "man of good birth and excellent education, endowed by nature with a phenomenal mathematical faculty." At the age of twenty-one, he published a text "on the binomial theorem which had a European vogue." This text won Moriarty the "mathematical chair of one of our smaller Universities," which would secure him a brilliant career. He also possessed "tendencies of the most diabolical kind." In this story, Arthur Conan Doyle also established Moriarty's role as the leader of London's criminal world.

"He is the Napoleon of crime, Watson. He is the organizer of half that is evil and nearly all that is undetected in the great city… He sits motionless like a spider in the centre of its web but that web has a thousand radiations and he knows well every quiver of each of them. He does little himself. He only plans."

Baring-Gould believed this detailed knowledge of Moriarty's career implied that Holmes possessed prior knowledge of him. He theorized that Moriarty's treatise on the binomial theorem was published in 1867. He also speculated that five years later, Squire Siger Holmes hired Professor Moriarty as a mathematical tutor for young Sherlock. This employment was brief, since Sherlock was unwilling to accept his tutor's teaching. This prompted Moriarty to depart from "Mycroft to return to his academic calling."

Upon his return to academia, Moriarty published his text *The Dynamics of An Asteroid.* It was also when he became known in the criminal underworld. These rumors and accusations forced him "to resign his chair and to come to London," where he became a teacher at a boarding school.

Baring-Gould also connected Professor Moriarty to the death of the American John Openshaw in "The Five Orange Pips." Openshaw sought Holmes's assistance in unraveling the meaning behind a threatening message he received that contained five orange pips. Despite the efforts of Holmes, John Openshaw was murdered. Baring-Gould believed that agents acting on orders from Moriarty performed the murder.

In 1974, Nicholas Meyer published the Sherlock Holmes pastiche, *The Seven Percent Solution: Being a Reprint from the Reminiscences of Doctor John H. Watson M.D.* Meyer is best known as the director of *Star Trek 2: The Wrath of Khan* and *Star Trek 6: The*

Undiscovered Country. In this novel, he built upon several of the theories popularized by Baring-Gould.

The first was the childhood home of Sherlock Holmes. As in *Sherlock Holmes of Baker Street: A Life of the World's First Consulting Detective*, the location of the Holmes family estate is North Riding in Yorkshire. It was here that Meyer contended that Mycroft Holmes was born. In this version, Squire Holmes was "a second son never due to inherit the family the estate at all by rights."

While the Holmes family lived in Yorkshire, the older brother of Squire Holmes died a widower. This prompted Squire Holmes to relocate to Sussex and move "his family into the old estate."

This description is inspired by a second theory concerning the childhood home of Sherlock Holmes. The Sherlockian Scholar Trevor H. Hall proposed in his essay "The Early Life of Sherlock Holmes" that the Holmes family originated in Sussex and that Sherlock Holmes was raised in East Sussex. The Holmes family estate would be located between the towns of Eastbourne and Brighton, where "the South Downs adjoined the sea." It was also where Sherlock had spent his childhood.

If the Holmes family resided in East Sussex, it would then be impossible for Holmes to have been raised in Yorkshire. Instead of being forced to choose between these two possible locations, Meyer designated Yorkshire as the birthplace of Sherlock Holmes and Sussex as his childhood home.

The Professor Moriarty in *The Seven Percent Solution* was inspired in part by *Sherlock Holmes of Baker Street: A Life of the World's First Consulting Detective*. In his novel, Meyer depicts Moriarty as the childhood mathematics tutor of Sherlock Holmes.

"Oh but I did," interrupted the professor, to my vast surprise.

"You did?"

"I did, indeed, and a most engaging young man he was, Master Sherlock."

"Master Sherlock?"

"Why, yes. I was his tutor in mathematics."

Nicholas Meyers theorized that Moriarty also tutored Mycroft Holmes.

"I see. And that is where you meet Holmes?"

"I taught both boys." Moriarty replied with more than a touch of pride "and brilliant lads they were too, both of 'em."

The most controversial theory proposed in *Sherlock Holmes of Baker Street: A Life of the World's First Consulting Detective* involves Irene Adler. Irene Adler is one of the most recognized characters in the Holmes Canon. However, like Professor Moriarty, she only appeared in one story. In "A Scandal in Bohemia," Miss Adler possessed a photograph of herself and Wilhelm Gottsreich Sigismond von Ormstein, the Grand Duke and heir to the throne of Bohemia. The two were involved in a brief romantic relationship. She planned to release this photograph to the London papers to prevent the Duke's upcoming wedding. The Grand Duke hired Holmes to locate and retrieve the photograph, although Holmes never succeeded in his task, for Irene Adler fled London with her new husband.

To Holmes there was only one Woman, "the late Irene Adler, of dubious and questionable memory." To him she represented the "whole of her sex." Adler also possessed an admiration for Sherlock Holmes and admitted herself flattered that she was an object of "interest to the celebrated Mister Sherlock Holmes."

Baring-Gould theorized that Holmes's admiration for Adler developed into a romantic interest after the events of "A Scandal in Bohemia." However, no reference is made to this relationship in "the Canon." The relationship was brief and occurred outside London. As such, Baring-Gould dated the relationship to 1892. In 1891, it was believed that Sherlock Holmes died at the hands of Professor Moriarty. Although Holmes survived, several high-ranking members of the professor's organization avoided the arrests conducted by Scotland Yard, which prompted Holmes to flee through Switzerland to Florence, Italy. For the next three years, he remained abroad under the name Sigerson.

Baring-Gould theorized that Holmes sailed from Italy to the country Montenegro. After his arrival, Holmes traveled to the capital city Cettigne. In 1891, this city possessed a population of three thousand inhabitants, which made it a place where a hunted man could "find a reasonable degree of security."

There he encountered Irene Adler, who was performing with a travelling opera company. The two became romantically involved. However, their relationship ended when Adler departed later that year. She boarded a steamer bound for the Italian coast prior to continuing across the Atlantic Ocean to the United States. Before her departure, Adler and Holmes consummated their relationship. During her voyage, she was pregnant with the child of Sherlock Holmes.

Baring-Gould postulated that as an adult, this child became Rex Stout's fictional private investigator Nero Wolfe. Several similarities exist between Sherlock Holmes and Nero Wolfe: both characters served as consultants to the governments of their respective countries; Holmes advised several inspectors of Scotland Yard, while Nero Wolfe often assisted the homicide detectives of the New York City police department; and during the Second World War, Nero Wolfe also served as a consultant for the Federal Bureau of Investigation. Both men were intellectuals and both often engaged in rigorous athletic activity.

As an adult, Nero Wolfe bore a closer resemblance to Mycroft Holmes. "The Greek Interpreter" describes Mycroft Holmes as being "much larger and stouter man than Sherlock. His body was absolutely corpulent, but his face though massive, had preserved something of the sharpness of the expression of which was so remarkable in that of his brother." Mycroft performed no exercise except for a daily walk from the Diogenes Club "into Whitehall every morning and back every evening."

Nero Wolfe and Mycroft Holmes also shared similar temperaments. In "The Greek Interpreter," Holmes describes his brother as lacking ambition.

"He will not even go out of his way to verify his own solutions, he would rather be considered wrong than take the trouble to prove himself right."

Nero Wolfe would not venture beyond West 35th Street while a case was in progress. Instead, he entrusted this work to either Archie Goodwin or to the men whom he employed as his agents.

This theory was inspired by one proposed by the scholar John D. Clark in the article "Some Notes Relating to A Preliminary Investigation into the Paternity of Nero Wolfe." This article was published in the *Baker Street Journal* in 1956. It was later reprinted in the collection *Sherlock Holmes by Gas Lamp: Highlights from the First Four Decades of the Baker Street Journal.*

Clark believed that in 1892 Holmes arranged for Irene Adler to board "one of the Italian steamers at Antivari." When she arrived in Italy, she bought passage across the Atlantic Ocean to "join her parents in New Jersey." Her son, whom she named Nero Wolfe, was born in Trenton, New Jersey "six months after his mother had left Montenegro." This placed the birth of the child in either the year 1892 or the year 1893. Sherlock Holmes remained behind in Montenegro to draw off her attackers.

In *Sherlock Holmes of Baker Street: A Life of The World's First Consulting Detective*, Baring-Gould speculated that Adler's flight was in response to the arrival of Colonel Sebastian Moran in Cettigne. This prompted Adler to flee to the United States. Before her departure, she left Holmes instructions that would lead him away from Montenegro towards London.

When Adler departed London in "A Scandal in Bohemia," she was married to the lawyer Geoffrey Norton, who was a member of a "respectful profession in a conformist age." Upon learning of his wife's previous criminal career, the marriage ended. As a result, the marriage lasted no "longer than two or three years." This freed Adler to become romantically involved with Sherlock Holmes. It also freed her to perform with "one of the smaller companies that toured through Eastern Europe" as an opera singer. This brought her to the opera house at Cettinge with the company, where she met Holmes.

After its publication in 1962, *Sherlock Holmes of Baker Street: A Life of the World's First Consulting Detective* revived warm praise from both literary critics and Sherlockian Scholars. The book was also a financial success. The success of this book led to the publication of *The Annotated Sherlock Holmes* in 1967. It also inspired Baring-Gould to write a second biography of a fictional character entitled *Nero Wolfe of West 35th Street: The Life and Times of America's Largest Detective*. It was released two years after Baring-Gould suffered a fatal stroke in 1967.

William S. Baring-Gould was a man who possessed great literary talent. He also possessed a deep passion for the world inhabited by Sherlock Holmes and Dr. John Watson. This led him to develop an extensive knowledge of both the Sherlock Holmes Canonical stories and the scholarly studies that they inspired. His passion is evident in the creation of his most influential work: *Sherlock Holmes of Baker Street: A Life of the World's First Consulting Detective*.

✗

Daniel DiQuinzio is a freelance writer residing in Essex County, New Jersey. He is a contributor to *Spotlight on Recovery* magazine along with *Foxtail* and *Unvealed* magazines. He is also a contributor to *Visionaros* magazine and a freelance correspondent for *The Patriot Times*, the newspaper of Springfield, New Jersey. He has worked as a freelance correspondent for *The Alternative Press* of Maplewood and South Orange and *The News Record* of Maplewood and South Orange. He is a graduate student at Seton Hall University. His nonfiction is forthcoming from *Visionarios* magazine and *Spotlight on Recovery* magazine.

A MEDIEVAL MYSTERY

by Peter James Quirk

Being the monarch of a modern European country is usually a secure, hereditary position. This, however, was not always the case. Czar Nicolas of Russia was assassinated with his entire family less than one hundred years ago. Queen Elizabeth of Great Britain, by contrast, is much respected and after more than fifty years on the throne, remains comfortable in her role as Britain's titular head of state. She sits down to her meals without fear of being poisoned and she sleeps at night without the remote possibility of being awakened by hostile troops and dragged off to the Tower of London.

Of course, life on the British throne was not always so harmonious. History informs us that during the Middle Ages, being the king of England was somewhat akin to being head of the Gambino crime family. Fortunately, Elizabeth's ancestors were up to the task. Indeed, the guiding principles of the Plantagenet kings, who presided over England for approximately three centuries (from 1215 to 1485), were remarkably similar to those of Lucky Luciano or John Gotti.

Their routine savagery peaked spectacularly in the late fifteenth century with a mysterious episode that could easily be the worst atrocity of the entire Plantagenet Dynasty: the disappearance and subsequent murder of the young Princes in the Tower. [The family tree on the following page shows only those members relevant to this narrative.]

The principal suspect in this medieval mystery is their uncle Richard (King Richard III). However, there is a compelling case, supported by a great many people, including eminent historians, for his innocence.

I was reminded of this crime while researching Richard's career and accomplishments for a novel. And I found that the record of his relatively short life—he was thirty-two when he was killed—is completely at odds with the universally-accepted version presented by William Shakespeare in his iconic play, "The Tragedy of King Richard III:"

"Now is the winter of our discontent
Made glorious summer by this sun of York" (I.i.1-2)

House of Plantagenet

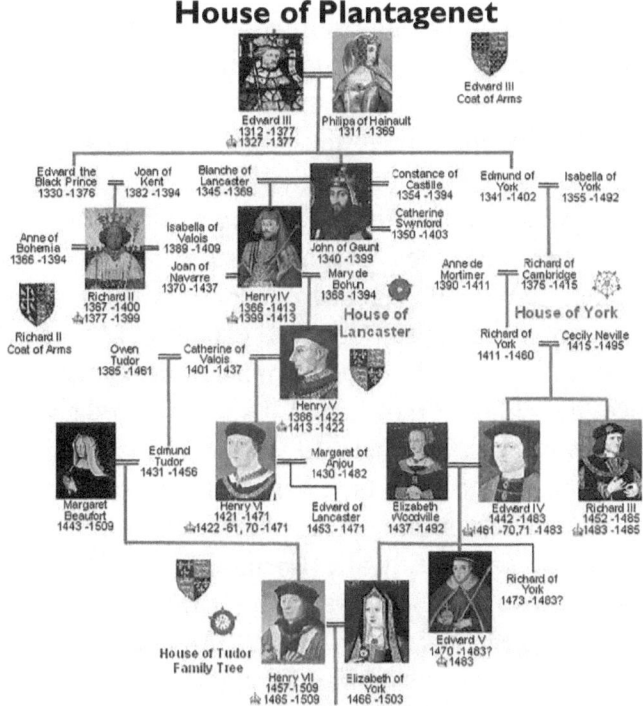

Unquestionably, the most monstrous of all the crimes attributed to him in that monumental work were the murders of his two young nephews, King Edward V and Richard, Duke of York—the Princes in the Tower:

"Shall I be plain? I wish the bastards dead,
And I would have it suddenly performed." (IV.ii.18-19)

This grisly double murder was even the subject of a crime novel written in 1951 by the distinguished Scottish mystery novelist Josephine Tey. In Tey's novel, her protagonist, Detective Inspector Alan Grant lies in a hospital bed with a broken leg. With nothing else to do, Grant mulls over pictures of historical figures brought to him by a friend to help alleviate his boredom.

When Grant draws up a favorable psychological study of one of the portrait's subjects, he is astounded to learn that this stately individual is no other than the arch-villain of English history, King Richard III. Grant then proceeds—with the timely assistance of nurses, friends, and an American student, who obtains research materials for him and discusses the case with him at his bedside—to prove that Richard is completely innocent of all charges. The title of the novel, "The Daughter of Time," is taken from a quote attributed to Galileo: "The truth is the daughter of time, not of authority."

So let us examine the known facts of this heinous crime beginning with the political situation: In the waning years of the Middle Ages, England was suffering through a series of fratricidal conflicts called the Wars of the Roses. During these wars, two branches of the Plantagenet family, the House of York (white rose) and the House of Lancaster (red rose), opposed each other for the throne.

The seeds of this struggle were sown a century before, when the Black Prince, the eldest son of King Edward III, died a year before his father. Edward III's death in 1377 placed the Black Prince's young son on the throne. This boy, King Richard II, was surrounded by envious and covetous uncles, notably John of Gaunt, Duke of Lancaster (third son of Edward III) and Richard, Duke of York, (fourth son of Edward III). Edward III, it must be remembered, was the fun-loving Plantagenet who, in 1338 declared himself the rightful king of France, thus precipitating the Hundred Year's War.

During Richard II's short unhappy reign, amongst other ill-considered decisions, he banished John of Gaunt's son, Henry Bolingbroke, from England. And when Bolingbroke gathered an army around him and returned to England in 1399, he defeated Richard II's forces in battle, imprisoned Richard and declared himself King Henry IV—much to the irritation and envy of his Yorkist cousins.

Flash forward to 1460 when Richard Plantagenet, Duke of York, (great-grandson of Edward III) took advantage of the then Lancastrian king's (Henry VI) mental illness, raised his standard and declared himself the rightful king of England. He was killed almost immediately, unfortunately, along with his second son Edmond, at the Battle of Wakefield.

Richard's eldest son, the eighteen-year-old Edward, immediately took up his father's cause and proved to be a military genius. He defeated the Lancastrians in a series of battles and assumed the throne as King Edward IV in 1461. Edward was forced to flee

England briefly in 1470, when some of his key allies switched to the Lancastrian side. When he returned some months later, however, with his young brother Richard, Duke of Gloucester (the future Richard III) at his side, he defeated the Lancastrians, executed Henry VI and ruled England in relative peace until his sudden death in 1483.

We now return to the Princes in the Tower, King Edward IV's sons: twelve-year old Edward (now King Edward V) and Richard, Duke of York (nine). Their uncle Richard was named Lord Protector under the provisions of the late king's will and as the Lord Protector, the loyal Richard had already begun preparations for the coronation of the young king when an influential bishop raised a crucial objection.

This bishop testified that King Edward—a notorious womanizer—had entered into a religious ceremony called "Troth Plight" with a young noblewoman before he married the boys' mother. This ceremony, which was legally binding, especially when followed by consummation—the noblewoman in question was still alive and able to testify—put King Edward's marriage to the Princes's mother in doubt, and thus the legitimacy of the Princes. This accusation, if substantiated, would make their uncle Richard, under the English rules of royal succession, the legal king.

Enter the English Parliament. Parliament had just witnessed several years of relative peace after more than a decade of civil war, and they were understandably fearful of placing a twelve-year-old boy upon the throne. So, given the opportunity to bypass the unproven boy for a tested warrior and administrator—Richard had fought loyally and successfully at his brother's side and governed the North of England prudently in his name—Parliament wrote Troth Plight into law and handed Richard the crown.

According to the Richard III Society—a group dedicated to restoring Richard's good name historically and theatrically—this law eliminated any motive Richard might have had to assassinate his nephews. It was certainly enough evidence to satisfy Josephine Tey's bed-ridden detective. However—and this is a big however—the fact remains that Richard sent the two boys to the Tower (of London), which at the time, was a royal residence and not a prison, but after August, 1483 they were neither seen nor heard from again. Richard, of course, had ample opportunity during his two-year reign to show they were alive and well and had never done so. (Their bodies were discovered a century later, buried under a staircase, during a renovation at the Tower.)

There is another leading suspect, however: Henry Tudor, a distant illegitimate Lancastrian with huge ambitions, who defeated and killed Richard III at the Battle of Bosworth Field:

"A horse, a horse, my kingdom for a horse" (V.iv.7)

This battle ended the Wars of the Roses and Henry claimed the throne as King Henry VII.

In order to unite the country and consolidate his position as king, Henry undertook to marry the Princess Elizabeth, oldest daughter of Edward IV and elder sister of the Princes in the Tower. But under the parliamentary Troth Plight law, Elizabeth was as illegitimate as her two brothers, so Henry had the law abolished, returning Elizabeth to her status as princess. They could now safely marry and reunite the two opposing Houses.

There was, of course, an inherent problem with that move: striking down Troth Plight not only legitimized Elizabeth, but the Princes too, and gave them both a more direct claim to the throne than that of Henry. This gave him a clear motive to have them removed—if indeed they were still alive.

So there you have it: two suspects, both members of an extremely bloodthirsty and ambitious clan and both with plenty of opportunity and motive to commit the crime and seize the prize—the prize being:

"This royal throne of kings, this scepter'd isle,

This earth of majesty, this seat of Mars," (King Richard II.II.i.40-41)

You be the judge!

✗

Peter James Quirk is an author, freelance writer, and outdoorsman who spends his winters skiing and snowboarding and his summers hiking, biking, and playing tennis. His novel *Trail of Vengeance* has a strong ski theme; indeed, the villain of the story is a disgraced ski instructor. Many of his stories, however, cover World War II and its aftermath. It is a fascinating if tragic period to explore, and the villains and heroes are so easy to find.

HAPPY BIRTHDAY, BIRTHDAY GIRL!

by Richard A. Lupoff

She didn't look so bad, she thought, peering at the image of herself in the back-bar mirror. The cobalt-blue coloring and the bottles of vodka and whiskey didn't hurt, and neither did the two, going-on-three, Lemon Drops that the bartender, what the hell was her name, not Mildred, Mildred's was the name of the bar, so not Mildred, no, Cissie, that was it, the Lemon Drops that Cissie kept serving up and Dorothy kept drinking down.

Not so bad for a broad observing her fortieth birthday. Observing, not celebrating, God no, not celebrating. The cake in the office with the big plastic 4-0 on top, everybody else seemed to be celebrating but Dorothy merely observed.

Still, look at the dame in the mirror. Face was still pretty good. Hair could use a bit of touching up, especially the roots, but she had that under control. Pretty much under control. Body could use a little work. She looked down at her chest. Not bad. Could use some trimming down. She had to admit that she was starting to sag just a little bit. She figured she'd only added a pound. One lousy pound. But a pound a year, starting when she was at her best, when she was twenty. Oh, the body she'd had then, the skin, the face, the hair…

She could get back to that or close to it anyway. She promised herself as much.

She lifted her glass and took a swallow of Lemon Drop. Man, that was delicious. Who invented these drinks, anyway? She opened her purse and searched for her wallet. Found it underneath her little Nikon. Nothing like the big Canon EOS she favored at work, or the Vivitar Waterproof she took on vacation last winter, but it was fun. She fished a twenty out of the wallet and dropped it on the bar.

Cissie took something that looked like a felt-tip marker and ran it over the bill, held it up to the tensor light over the cash register, nodded and rang up the sale.

When she slid Dorothy's change to her, Dorothy asked what that had been about.

Cissie said, "Checking for queer, m'dear. We got a bulletin from the Feds about phony bills, especially twenties. I found two of 'em last week, and even a fake Canadian twenty today. And we have to eat those, you know. So we're being extra careful."

Somebody had left an out-of-town paper on the bar stool next to Dorothy's. Paper had a headline about the Red Wings and the Bruins, whoever they were. She picked it up and looked at the weather forecast. Cloudy and warmer. Not here, it wasn't. Cloudy all right. But hardly warmer. Snowflakes had been drifting down when she left the office and the breeze coming off the lake was like ice. A good thing Mildred's was so close, she could walk there before she got more than a few stray flakes on her hair and the shoulders of her coat.

Cissie the bartender—Dorothy had once heard a customer call her a mixologist and Cissie had practically had a fit—Cissie the bartender had turned on some music. It was a CD that Dorothy had heard before. All Gershwin tunes.

Embrace me, you sweet embraceable you.

Right.

Some guy wearing a hound's tooth jacket came out of the rest room and hoisted himself onto the stool next to Dorothy's. He said, "You can keep it if you want it." He wore thick eyeglasses with a bifocal line across the middle and boring-looking plastic frames. He smelled faintly of cigar smoke. A loser.

She gave him a WTF look.

"The paper," he said. He tapped the newspaper with a stubby finger. "That's my paper, but I'm through with it. You can have it."

Embrace me, you irreplaceable you.

Dorothy half-turned toward the guy.

He waggled a finger at Cissie. Cissie nodded encouragingly and he said, "Would you mind turning the light away?" He indicated the miniature tensor light on top of the cash register. "It's—my eyes are sensitive and…." He made a vague, helpless gesture.

Cissie said, "Sure." She turned the light away from him.

Dorothy started to say something about the newspaper, wondering if it was a pick-up line or if the guy was just being decent. If he was a pick-up artist he was the world's most inept practitioner of the art.

That was when she saw Carter sitting at a table with a woman. What a coincidence. Carter was supposed to be out of town on business, and here he was in Chicago sitting with a frowsy blond bitch having a drink.

Of all the gin joints in the world, Dorothy thought.

That son of a bitch, she thought.

She turned away quickly so her back was to Carter and the frowsy bitch. She could see them clearly in the back-bar mirror. The blond bitch wasn't so frowsy after all. In fact she was classier than Dorothy had thought, well turned out and at least ten years younger than Dorothy. Old enough to have been around the block a couple of times but young enough to still have what Dorothy had misplaced somewhere along the way.

You'd think the bastard would have had the decency to stick around for Dorothy's birthday. They could have had a meal in a nice joint, gone back to her place or to his for a nightcap and some laughs. How often did a girl turn forty anyhow?

Carter and the bimbo were leaning over their little table, laughing at something. They hadn't seen Dorothy, that was obvious. They were holding hands like a pair of shy teenagers just figuring out which way was up. With their free hands they lifted their glasses. She couldn't tell what the bimbo was drinking but it was in a Martini glass. She knew what Carter drank. Jack Daniels neat.

They clinked glasses. The bimbo sipped at her drink. Carter, the son of a bitch, knocked back his JD like a desert rat getting his first taste of water in a week. They both put their glasses down. While Dorothy watched, Carter slipped his free hand under the table and reached for the bimbo. She was wearing a skirt, Dorothy could tell that. Carter moved his hand.

Son of a bitch! That was too much. Bad enough what was going on, but rubbing her nose in it was more than any woman could take.

Dorothy pushed herself away from the bar. The out-of-town paper went flying. Her bar stool tipped over backwards and the guy on the next stool half-reached, half-dived for it and caught it before it crashed to the floor.

Dorothy covered the distance to the table where Carter and the bimbo were carrying on in a few angry strides. She had her Lemon Drop glass in her hand.

Carter stood up. He held his hand toward Dorothy. The hand that he'd just withdrawn from under the bimbo's skirt. He was sweating. He was wearing a classy gray suit and a white shirt with a button-down collar and a tie striped in quiet colors. He said, "Dorothy—"

She said, "You fucker!"

He said, "Dorothy." He turned to the bimbo, looking down at her. He said, "Marianne." He looked back at Dorothy. He said, "Dorothy, this is my friend Mari—"

She smelled something, a combination of some flowery, young girl perfume and harsh female musk. She felt sick.

She threw what was left of her third Lemon Drop, half a Lemon Drop, in his face. She felt like a fool, a character in some stupid melodrama, some amateur community theater production of a cheap melodrama.

Her drink was dripping off Carter's face, mostly landing on his suit, some of it splashing on the table, none of it hitting Marianne the bimbo.

Carter raised his hand, a gesture halfway between the sign that a traffic cop would make to stop cars and the gesture that a kid in a stupid game of Cowboys and Indians would make when he was stuck being an Indian.

Dorothy heard a sound that was somewhere between a roar and a shriek and smashed her Lemon Drop glass on the table top and thrust it at Carter and raked it down his cheek leaving a trail that turned red and spurted blood.

Marianne the bimbo screamed and jumped up and grabbed Carter.

Dorothy thrust the broken glass at Carter's chest. It hit the lapel of his suit and Dorothy's hand hit the suit. The jagged edge of the glass sliced into her wrist and more blood spurted. She dropped the glass and it landed on the table and bounced and fell on the floor.

Don't be a naughty papa, come to baby, come to baby, do.

There were a couple of napkins on the table and she grabbed a couple of them and held them against her wrist to stop the bleeding.

Her purse was hanging from her arm and she swung it at Marianne the bimbo and missed. She turned around and ran from Mildred's.

The door was heavy, padded to keep street sounds out. Dorothy had to lean on it with her shoulder and shove to get it open. The cold air and noise hit her like a fist. She turned around and looked back inside. There was a small window in the middle of the door, round like a ship's porthole, the glass thick and heavy. Through the window she could see confusion. Carter was standing where he had been, holding a napkin against his face. It was too dark inside Mildred's for Dorothy to tell whether the napkin was showing blood or not. Marianne the bimbo was dancing around Carter as if she didn't know what to do, her hands fluttering in confusion, first here then there. Cissie had come around the bar. Dorothy saw her cast one quick glance at the door but they didn't make eye contact. Instead Cissie turned and ran toward Carter and Marianne the bimbo.

There were a couple of other patrons in the place. They were milling around in confusion. The guy who'd told Dorothy she could keep his newspaper was still sitting on his bar stool as if he didn't know what to do. A classic poster of Joan Crawford as Mildred Pierce was the only decoration in the place.

Dorothy shoved her hand inside the pocket of the heavy, dark coat she'd been wearing. She still had the napkins wrapped around her wrist. She didn't think she was bleeding any more.

The sidewalk was crowded with workers who'd stayed past quitting time and were on their way home, and with people headed out for the evening.

Dorothy had been walking as fast as the crowd would permit. Now she slowed down. She was short of breath. Each time she let out a lungful of air it turned to mist in front of her. The air she took back in felt good. It tasted good.

She reached the corner and turned to the right and kept on walking. This was a mixed neighborhood of shops, offices and high rise apartment buildings. She reached the next corner and turned again, kept going again, reached another corner. Eventually she realized that she was about to head back to Mildred's.

She turned and headed in the opposite direction. She walked through the cold night until she came to a movie theater. She bought a ticket and went in and sat through part of some movie. She had no idea what she was watching.

She got up and made her way to the rest room. She turned on the cold water and let it run over the cut on her wrist. The skin turned fish-belly white around the cut. It wasn't much more than a scratch. She threw the napkins she'd brought from Mildred's in a waste container. She blotted the wound with a paper towel. A couple of drops of blood oozed from it.

She looked at her wristwatch. It was getting late. She felt sick to her stomach.

She left the theater and walked some more. She walked until she stood in front of her building. She went inside and took the self-service elevator up to her floor. She used her key and went inside her apartment. She smelled something.

She dropped her coat on the sofa and headed for her bedroom. It was down a short hallway from the living room. She pushed the door open and saw something on her bed. The comforter was drawn over the bed and all she could see was a lump the size of a man with an extra rise in it. It made her think of what a man's body would look like as he lay on his back with an erection but the rise was at the wrong place.

She pulled back the comforter and looked at the man lying on her bed. It was Carter. Carter Hanson. The jagged cut on his cheek had stopped bleeding but blood had run down his cheek and onto Dorothy's best bedding.

He was nude except for a pair of lace-edged, bright red panties and matching brassiere. The panties had been pulled up to cover his hips and pubes, their elastic top stretched and squeezing his belly. The ends of the brassiere, designed to hook between the wearer's breasts, lay open. Dorothy recognized the garments as her own. Carter had bought them for her from a website and asked her to dance for him, wearing them and then removing them.

The tent in the comforter had been made by the handle of a heavy kitchen knife, Dorothy's best knife. It was covered with blood. She reached for it and tried to pull it from Carter's chest. It must have been plunged in with great force, probably stuck in bone, maybe his sternum, maybe caught between two ribs.

In order to get the knife out Dorothy had to kneel on the bed next to Carter and grab the knife with both hands and lean backwards with all her weight while she tugged with both hands. When the knife came loose it did so suddenly and Dorothy tumbled backwards, landing on her back on the carpet next to the bed. The knife flew out of her hands and bounced off the drapes and fell to the floor.

She pulled herself to her feet. Her hands were smeared with blood. She went to the bathroom and rinsed her hands off, washing them with hot water and soap. That made her cut start to bleed again and she blotted it dry, found a box of adhesive bandages in the medicine cabinet and bandaged the cut. She dropped the now-bloody towel in the laundry hamper.

She took a deep breath. She stood looking at herself in the mirror. Her hair was a mess.

She went back into the bedroom, walked past the bed with a quick glance at Carter Hanson lying dead, still half-covered with her expensive comforter.

Back in the living room she picked up the telephone and called the emergency number. She got a recorded message that made her laugh until she realized she was verging on hysterics so she sat down and worked her way through a telephone maze until she got a live human being and said, "I just got home and there's a man in my bed and he's dead. Somebody stabbed him and he's dead."

Suddenly the person on the other end of the line started to sound interested.

She laughed again when the police arrived and she had to buzz them up because her building didn't have a doorman and there was nobody in the lobby to let them in. They hit the buzzer for her apartment and she buzzed them in and in a couple of minutes they were at her door and she was letting them in and they were milling around, mainly looking at the scene in her bedroom.

One of the police was a female officer. She said she was a detective and told Dorothy her name but it whizzed past Dorothy's ear. She couldn't have told you the woman's name five seconds after she'd heard it. But she told the officer her name, Dorothy Doe, and extended her hand.

The female officer looked startled but she accepted Dorothy's hand and shook it.

"Dorothy Doe," the female officer said, "as in John Doe?"

Dorothy said, "Yes."

Another officer, male, came out of the bedroom and leaned over the female officer. They engaged in a brief, whispered conversation. They took turns looking at Dorothy and at each other and casting glances toward the bedroom.

The male officer said, "Miss Doe?"

Dorothy said, "Miz."

"Of course. Will you come with us, please?"

They led her, the male officer at one elbow and the female officer at the other, into the bedroom.

Carter Hanson was still lying on the bed, staring at the ceiling, the same ceiling that Dorothy had seen many times, looking upward over Carter Hanson's shoulder.

Dorothy said, "He's dead." It was twenty-five per cent question, seventy-five per cent statement.

The two officers ignored that. The male officer said, "Do you know this man?"

Dorothy said, "It's my birthday, you know."

The officers ignored that. "Do you know this man?"

"Is he dead?"

"Yes ma'am," the male officer said. "We'll have to wait for the medical examiner to certify as much, but it's pretty obvious. He's dead."

The female officer took Dorothy's hands in her own. She said, "Do you know who he is?"

"Carter Hanson."

"You knew him."

Dorothy smiled. "I knew him."

"Did he have a key to your apartment?"

"We both did. He had mine, I had his."

She heard a commotion from the living room. She turned to see what was going on. She ought to see what was happening. She didn't want strangers wandering into her apartment. The two officers, male and female, held her. The female officer still had Dorothy's two hands in her own hands. The male officer closed strong fingers around her biceps.

More people came into the bedroom. The two officers took Dorothy back to the living room. They let her sit on the sofa. The female officer sat beside her. The male officer stood a few feet away. He paced nervously. He was a big man. He wore a brown suit and a yellow shirt and a tie with little footballs all over it. He kept buttoning and unbuttoning his suit jacket. When he buttoned it, it pulled. Then he would unbutton it again for a minute.

He must have gained weight since he bought the suit. Dorothy figured that his wife wanted him either to lose some weight or to take the suit to a tailor and have it let out so the button wouldn't tug that way.

There was a bright flash of light from the bedroom, then another. Dorothy blinked, then decided that a police technician was using a flash camera to record the situation in the bedroom. There was even a term for it. She thought about it, then it came to her. Crime scene photos. That was it. Crime scene photos.

Another man in a suit walked out of the bedroom. He squatted on the carpet in front of the sofa. Dorothy felt oddly comforted. The female detective was beside her. The male in the too-tight brown suit had seated himself heavily on her other side. He had exhaled loudly as he landed on the couch. Really, his wife would have to work on him.

The newcomer wore a dark blue suit, solid in color. White shirt. Dark red tie, some semi-glossy material, more likely silk than an artificial fiber. Good haircut. Air of authority.

He squatted on the gray wall-to-wall carpet in front of Dorothy, reached into a jacket pocket and produced a pair of metal-framed eyeglasses. Rectangular lenses. He started to speak but Dorothy got there first.

"Please, you'll be uncomfortable. There are plenty of chairs."

The man smiled. He leaned toward the brown-suited man and said a few words, then made a gesture with his head.

The brown-suited man got up and walked back into the bedroom. In a minute he returned carrying a small device. He sat down beside Dorothy and studied the device, touched it a few times, then nodded to the blue-suited man.

The blue-suited man had accepted Dorothy's invitation, drawn up a chair from the dining table and seated himself.

"I'm Detective Inspector Edward Goodman, City Police Department. The time is—" he looked at his wristwatch—"twenty-two twenty-five hours." He added the date and the address of Dorothy's building and the apartment number. He said, "I am talking with—" and then he stopped and asked Dorothy to identify herself.

She gave her full name. Her voice sounded calm and matter-of-fact. She was surprised to hear herself sounding like a woman in control of herself. She knew that a reaction to the sight in her bedroom would surely come, but up to this moment it had not.

Inspector Goodman said, "This will be a very brief interview. It is conducted in the presence of two police officers, one male and one female." He gave their names.

"Dorothy—may I call you Dorothy?"

She nodded.

"This is an informal interview. You understand that you are not arrested or detained. We are merely trying to gather some information. Do you understand that?"

Dorothy nodded.

Inspector Goodman indicated the recording device. He said, "Please."

Dorothy took his meaning. She said, "Yes."

Goodman nodded again, waited.

Dorothy said, "Yes, I understand."

"A man is lying on the bed in this apartment. He appears to be deceased. The examiner is making a determination now." He nodded as if he'd asked himself a question and answered affirmatively.

"Do you know who that man is, Dorothy?"

She nodded, then remembered about the recording device and said, "Yes." She was surprised to find that she had trouble getting the word out. Again she said, "Yes, I know him."

She began to cry. She looked around frantically, her hands waving as if they had minds of their own, looking for a handkerchief, tears suddenly running down her face.

The female police officer produced a handkerchief and handed it to her. She held it to her face, felt her body jerk in a sob, another, then drew a deep breath and offered the handkerchief back to the officer who declined to accept it.

Inspector Goodman said, "Who is the man in the other room?"

"Carter Hanson."

"You know him personally?"

She smiled and a harsh giggle escaped her throat, hurting as it did so, like an involuntary cough when you're just getting over a nasty sore throat. She looked toward a nearby window. There were drapes, dark floral-patterned drapes, but they were drawn back to provide a view of the city. It was very dark outside but the city lights provided a glittering backdrop for falling snowflakes.

"Dorothy?" Inspector Goodman prompted.

"I knew him," Dorothy said. She felt herself nodding, actually bobbing her head up and down in a short, quick arc. She stopped that. "I knew him. And he knew me."

"You're sure of his identity." It was half a question, half a statement. "Would you—I know this will be difficult, Dorothy, but Officer McKibbon will stay with you." He indicated the female officer seated beside Dorothy. "This may be just a formality but we need you to take a look at the deceased and confirm the identification you've given us."

Dorothy managed an ironic smile. How smoothly Goodman had slid into that nice, impersonal language. *The deceased.* Not *the corpse.* Not *the body.* Not *the stiff.* Not *the departed.* No, that would be funeral director talk. *The departed.* How to talk about death without mentioning death. Oh, better even than *the departed,* Inspector Goodman, how about *the dear departed.*

Quiet organ music in the background, soft lighting, stained glass windows, tasteful floral displays, maybe just a touch of incense in the air. Maybe she was wasting her time working at *Dog Lover's Digest.* And she didn't even own a dog. She ought to be doing photo layouts for some funeral directors' trade journal. She—

"Miss Doe?"

She blinked.

It was the funeral director, no, the detective, Inspector Goodman, what a lovely name for a cop.

"Miss Doe? Are you all right?"

She blinked.

"Would you like a glass of water? Galloway, get Miss Doe a glass of water."

The cop in the too-tight brown suit stood up and headed for the kitchen. He must have scoped out the apartment while Dorothy wasn't looking. Otherwise, how did he know where the kitchen was?

He came back with one of Dorothy's kitchen glasses and held it for her. She took a sip and nodded gratefully. He stood there looking uncertain of what to do, holding the glass of water.

Inspector Goodman said, "Please. If you think you can handle this."

Dorothy nodded affirmatively. She stood up. She felt the female cop, McKibbon, holding her by the elbow, helping her to stand, steering her back toward the bedroom.

The room was still bustling with strangers. A couple of uniformed cops, a man and a woman in medical whites. Another civilian-in-a-suit, Dorothy figured him for a medical examiner.

Inspector Goodman stood next to the bed, Dorothy beside him, Officer McKibbon beside her. Goodman asked again, "Do you know this person?"

"Yes."

"Please identify him."

"His name is Carter Hanson."

"Do you know where he lives? Lived," Goodman corrected himself.

Dorothy nodded, gave Carter's address.

"What was your relationship with Carter Hanson?"

"We were…" She stopped, gathered herself. "He used to stay over some nights, or I would stay at his place. We talked about moving in, sharing an apartment."

"You were intimate?"

She couldn't resist another sardonic grin. *Intimate. Jesus, we used to fuck like minks.*

"Dorothy? Miss Doe?"

"We were intimate."

"Are those your garments?" Goodman asked. "Did Hanson like to dress in women's undergarments?"

"They're mine. He never wore my clothes. My underwear. They wouldn't fit. He was much too big."

She found herself reaching out toward *the deceased. The body. The corpse. The stiff.*

Goodman took her wrist. Blood showed through the bandage she'd put on her cut. "I see you've been hurt. What happened?"

"Nothing. I just scratched myself. It's nothing."

Goodman nodded toward a uniformed officer holding a clear plastic bag. Dorothy turned her head, saw that her best kitchen knife was in the bag.

"Is that yours?" Goodman asked.

The uniformed cop stepped closer to them, held the bag so she could see it clearly but not so close that she could touch it.

"That's my best knife."

Goodman asked, "Did you kill Mr. Hanson?"

"No."

"What would it mean if we find your fingerprints on the knife? If we test your hands, what if we find traces of Mr. Hanson's blood?"

"When I found him," Dorothy said. "When I came home and found him, he was under the comforter. I pulled it back and saw the knife. I pulled it out of his chest. It was stuck tight. I had to pull hard but I got it out. Then I washed my hands."

"That's your statement? He was—like that when you got home—and you removed the knife? Why did you do that?"

She shook her head. "I don't know. I just did."

"Did you think he might still be alive?"

"I don't know. I just—I saw the knife and I pulled it out. I got blood on my hands. I washed my hands and called emergency."

Goodman said, "All right." He nodded to McKibbon and Galloway and they led her back to the living room.

"Would you be willing to come to the precinct with us and give a statement? And would you mind if we take a DNA sample?"

She felt a light shudder pass through her body.

"The DNA sample," Goodman said, "it's painless. Non-invasive. We just ask you to let us take a swab of the inside of your cheek. Doesn't hurt, takes a second, that's all."

"Am I under arrest?"

"No." He shook his head. Again, "No. We'd just like your help. You're not under arrest."

"Can I come back here after?"

Goodman hesitated. "I'm not sure that would be wise. Might be a good idea to stay with a friend tonight. Or a family member. Is there anyone…" He left the question hanging.

She shook her head. "No, I—I'm from Buffalo. Buffalo, New York. I'm a photographer. I came here to take a job at *Dog Lover's Digest*. Shooting layouts of show-dogs. The people I work with—colleagues. But I don't think…" This time she left the sentence hanging.

"We can put you up at a hotel, then."

"You're sure I'm not under arrest."

"Absolutely."

✗   ✗   ✗   ✗

Officer McKibbon, the female cop, stayed in Goodman's work space with Goodman while he questioned Dorothy. The surroundings were much like an office in an up-to-date building. The kind of room that lower-middle management got. Functional furniture. Couple of trophies and mementos for decorations. No outside windows. Probably Goodman would get an office with an outside window with his next promotion.

They went over the same ground that they'd covered at Dorothy's apartment. Then Goodman asked her to review her whole day and night.

She noticed that they weren't just recording the interview, they were making a video of it. No hot lights, though. Must be pretty good equipment to get a decent image by available light. No rubber hoses, nobody blowing cigarette smoke in her face. Nothing like the hardboiled movies. Just Goodman asking questions in his polite, friendly voice, and McKibbon sitting there quietly just in case.

Just in case what?

Just in case things went badly and Dorothy wanted to get lawyered up and started howling about inappropriate sexual contact during the interrogation.

"Your co-workers at—what was the name of the magazine? Oh, *Dog Lover's Digest*, yes—they'll vouch for you?"

"I was there until around six-thirty. I wasn't the last to leave, either. And you have to sign in and out of the building anyway. Maybe they're being paranoid but..." She let the thought slip away.

Goodman said, "Okay, that's good news. We'll check up on it. And then?"

She told him about stopping at Mildred's after work.

Goodman wanted to know if that was her usual practice.

No. It had been a rough day. Ellen Stein was complaining about a spread that Dorothy turned in. Said the colors were all wrong, the layout looked like something out of a Sixties teenage mag, the sizing was off. Somehow she'd got through it but instead of leaving a little after five o'clock as she'd planned, she had to do the whole layout over and that took an hour and a half of unpaid overtime.

And with Carter in Detroit on business she'd been planning to go straight home and pig out on comfort food and turn on an Ella Fitzgerald CD and climb in bed with a thick P. D. James novel.

"But you didn't," Goodman said.

"By the time I left the doghouse—that's what we call the office—I was too pissed off to—I—anyway, I couldn't face an empty apartment. I'd be bouncing off the walls. So I stopped at Mildred's."

"That isn't a lesbian bar, is it?"

Dorothy saw Officer McKibbons' eyebrows jump when Goodman asked that.

"No."

"Anyone there know you? Did you talk to anyone who might remember?"

"Some guy tried to pick me up. Maybe not. I was looking at a paper and he said it was his. Nothing else. But Cissie knows me. Bartender. We're not BFF's or anything, but we talk now and then."

"And then?"

"That's when I saw Carter and the blond bimbo playing feel-me-up. In the mirror. I was sitting at the bar. They were at a table. I saw them in the mirror."

Goodman made an encouraging sound, somewhere between a hum and a grunt. It translated as *keep going.* Dorothy did. When she came to the part about the broken Martini glass Goodman raised his hand the way Carter had raised his hand when Dorothy confronted him at Mildred's.

"Is that when you cut yourself?"

Dorothy held up her bandaged hand like a school kid doing show-and-tell.

"I guess I went nuts," Dorothy said. "He was supposed to be in Detroit and here he was playing grab-my-crotch with this bimbo. If Ellen hadn't been such a bitch about the photo layout I would have been home by then thinking he was in Detroit and hoping he'd call me up just to say good-night and there he was with his hand up that bitch's skirt, laughing at me. So I let him have it with the martini glass."

She was panting. Must be some dead air, nothing happening on-screen in the video. Wouldn't pull much on YouTube unless they edited it down.

Finally Goodman asked her to go on.

She told him about the movie.

Did she remember which theater? What picture?

She shook her head.

He suggested—by any chance had she saved her ticket stub?

She had no idea. Probably threw it away. She never saved them. She wasn't a pack rat.

"And then?"

"Then I went home. I was feeling better. My wrist was throbbing a little where I cut myself but it's really just a scratch. I thought about what I'd done to Carter. I knew I got his face and he'd show the result for a while but I didn't think I'd got his eye and I was glad. I was starting to feel a little better about the bastard."

"Better," Goodman said. "Would you like a drink of water? Are you hungry? You didn't have dinner tonight, did you? Did you have a snack at the movie?"

"Water, yes."

Goodman nodded and McKibbon got up and got a glass and handed it to Dorothy.

"After the movie," Goodman prompted, "what did you do?"

Dorothy swallowed some water. It tasted pretty good, better than she'd expected.

She said, "Nothing."

"Nothing?"

"I went home." She shrugged. "It was getting late. I was starting to come down. I guess I'd had an adrenaline rush at Mildred's and the movie—it wasn't anything interesting, I don't even remember what it was, something about an airplane crash and survivors, I don't know, I wasn't paying attention. The movie ended and I went home."

"How did you do that?"

"What? Oh, go home? I walked. I've always been a good walk-er. The air felt good. I don't mind a few snowflakes. I'm a Buffalo girl. You think it snows here, you ought to spend a winter in Buffalo, you'll learn about snow."

Goodman said, "I'm sorry. It's getting late and you must be very tired, and we're digressing. We can wrap this up for now and you can get some rest."

"Yes, please." As if the power of suggestion had taken her over, Dorothy felt suddenly very, very tired.

"You got home and went into the bedroom and found Mr. Hanson in your bed."

"Under the comforter."

"Under your comforter."

"I saw the tent where the knife was. I pulled back the comforter and pulled out the knife. Got blood on my hands. Washed it off. Phoned you."

Goodman nodded. "I think we're caught up. You've been very helpful, Miss Doe."

"Miz."

"I'm very sorry. Of course. Officer McKibbon will give you a ride to a hotel. Do you need anything? Maybe stop at a drugstore and pick up a few toiletries. On the department." He smiled.

Dorothy stood up.

"Oh, one more thing," Goodman said. "I think you mentioned that Mr. Hanson didn't usually wear your underwear. Is that correct?"

"Yes."

"Do you have any idea why he was wearing it tonight?"

"No."

McKibbon took her by the elbow and steered her toward the door.

Before she reached the door Goodman said, "You won't leave town, will you? In case we need to speak with you again."

She was almost too tired to answer. "Can I—can I go to work tomorrow?"

Goodman said, "Absolutely. I mean, if you feel up to it. I'm sure your employer will understand if you need to rest up. But that's up to you, Miss Doe."

⚹ ⚹ ⚹ ⚹

Officer Galloway drove and waited in the unmarked car. He waited while Dorothy and Detective McKibbon went into an all-night drugstore and Dorothy bought a few necessities. They got back in the car and Galloway drove them to a nondescript downtown hotel.

McKibbon handled registration. It was obvious that she and the desk clerk knew each other. Dorothy inferred that the police department had a standing arrangement with the hotel. Nobody asked why Dorothy was checking in with only a drugstore package for luggage. The two women rode up in the elevator together.

The room was functional. The bed looked comfortable. Dorothy put her new toiletries in the bathroom. She faced the female cop. "Officer McKibbon—" she began.

"Actually it's Sergeant but you might as well call me Jackie. Jacqueline to be fancy, but I prefer Jackie."

"Are you going to stay with me?"

"Only if you want me to. You should be safe here. You don't think whoever killed Carter Hanson is after you, do you?"

"I thought—I thought I was the suspect."

"Not for me to say. Inspector Goodman is in charge of the investigation."

Dorothy was looking around the room, not certain what she was looking for but somehow not quite sure she felt safe.

McKibbon—Jackie, Dorothy reminded herself—must have sensed Dorothy's unease. "We use this hotel when we need to put someone up."

"Then I'm not under arrest." Goodman had told her as much, but she wanted to hear it again.

Jackie shook her head. "You are not."

"Is this—what do you call it—protective custody?"

"No, Dorothy. Not that either. It's just—call it a courtesy. Your apartment is a crime scene. No way you could stay there tonight. The medical examiner will remove the victim. Evidence techs will be all over the place, dusting for fingerprints, looking for blood samples, taking photos. They don't want you there and you don't want to be there, believe me. I'm afraid you've seen the last of that comforter on your bed. It was beautiful, too."

McKibbon smiled.

Dorothy said, "It came from Marshall Fields. You remember the big sale just before Macy's took it over. I'll never set foot in that store again. Somebody ought to blow it up!"

Dorothy stopped. She put her hand to her mouth. "I didn't mean that. I wouldn't really—"

Jackie McKibbon actually laughed. It was the first laugh Dorothy had heard since she left the doghouse—how many hours ago? She looked at her Lambretta Cielo watch. It was after midnight. No wonder she was so tired.

Jackie said, "Just between you and me, Dorothy, I felt the same way. Some people have no respect for tradition." She went over to the window and pulled the curtains back.

Dorothy looked past her at the city. She'd loved this town since the day she arrived. The energy, the excitement of the big city combined with the earnestness of the Midwest. She'd felt at home from that day until—tonight.

Had Jackie been reading her mind?

"Unless you want me to stay, Dorothy, I think I'll head out now. We have the hotel number and your work number. You'll probably hear from Inspector Goodman in the next couple of days."

"When can I get back into my apartment?"

"Call the precinct. Or just call Inspector Goodman or me." She wrote a couple of phone numbers on a business card and handed it to Dorothy. "You can probably get back in tomorrow if you want to, but phone us first."

She went to the door.

"You're sure you're all right? Need some food, anything else?"

"I'll sleep."

Once McKibbon was gone Dorothy checked out the room. If the police put people up here regularly the place might be bugged. She couldn't find anything. *But then,* she thought, *what if the place was bugged? What would they hear, snores?* She smiled to herself.

She brushed her teeth and stripped down to her underpants and climbed into bed. Suddenly she wasn't just tired, she was sore in every part of her body. She watched a video playing on the ceiling, herself in Mildred's, the pick-up artist claiming ownership of the newspaper, the Gershwin tune.

I love all the many charms about you.

Suddenly, with no warning, she was crying.

Above all I want my arms about you.

That bastard. How could he do that to her? Who in hell was the blond bimbo? Something with an M. Mikey, Martha, Marianne.

That was it. Marianne. What did she have that Dorothy didn't have?

Had she told Goodman about Marianne? She tried to remember her interrogation. He hadn't been nasty, no third degree tactics. Was there even such a thing, or was that just the stuff of comic books and gangster movies?

Why was Carter wearing her bra and panties?

She hated the son of a bitch.

She loved the son of a bitch.

She screamed once, then felt better, stopped crying, clicked off the video on the ceiling.

⚡ ⚡ ⚡ ⚡

She ordered breakfast from room service; it came with a copy of the World's Greatest Newspaper. There was a one-paragraph story about Carter Hanson's murder, buried near the bottom of an inside page of the local news section. That was all the space that the crime rated.

She got dressed. She'd bought a fresh pair of panties at the drugstore—they sold everything except drugs there—but other-wise wore the same outfit she'd had on when she left the office a million years ago or maybe yesterday.

She got to the office at midmorning. Joanna the receptionist gave her a questioning look but said nothing as she hung up her winter coat. Ellen Stein came out of her office and asked Dorothy to come in. She shut the door. She asked Dorothy if she wanted to take the day off. The issue was about ready to go to bed. Avril could clean up the loose ends.

Dorothy said she'd rather stay. She went to her desk and opened and closed drawers. She felt light-headed. She drifted through the rest of the morning. At noontime she asked Avril if she'd mind finishing up. She got her coat off the rack and left.

She made her way to Carter Hanson's building. She wondered if the police had sealed his apartment, too, as a crime scene. Probably not. After all, nothing had happened there. The whole sequence of events had started at Mildred's and ended at Dorothy's.

Carter had lived in posher surroundings than Dorothy. There was a uniformed doorman to contend with, and an elevator operator. They both recognized her, both of them murmured a few incoherent words to her, neither of them said anything about the police, neither of them tried to stop her from making her way to Carter's apartment.

She stepped inside and the heavy apartment door slammed itself behind her like the lid coming down on a heavy coffin. She shivered.

The apartment was familiar enough. She'd been there—how many times? There was something in the air. A stale odor. Carter must not have been home for the past few days. He'd said he was going to Detroit on business. Dorothy realized that she didn't really know what his business was. Whenever she asked he told her it was pretty boring, nothing as exciting and creative as hers. Being a glamour photographer, now, that was something to be excited about.

She laughed then. Photographing smug society matrons posing with their pampered pups was a living but it wasn't why she'd moved all those miles and taken this job. Dorothy was saving her money. Once she had enough put away she was going to give her notice at *Dog Lover's Digest*, tell Ellen Stein that Avril Freeman was ready to take over her job, and set up a studio of her own. She had enough contacts to make it as a freelance. She'd have to hustle, but the thought of never having to shoot another prize poodle with its coat cut into pompoms and a hundred dollar ribbon on top of its head kept her going.

She circled the living room, pulled back the drapes and peered out at the city. The sky was gray this morning. She'd been in such a fog, she hadn't even noticed what kind of day it was until now. She could see a vague, milky brightness where the sun was trying to break through the clouds. A few snowflakes were drifting down again. There hadn't been much snow this winter, and the few sizable storms had given way to brief thaws. The streets were clear.

She walked into the kitchen, opened the fridge. Nothing remarkable there. Somebody would have to clean it out, though. Carter wasn't coming back. Nothing much in the cupboard. A few cans of soup, some veggies, packages of pasta. Carter liked elbow macaroni, that was his favorite. Had been his favorite, Dorothy reminded herself.

She put her purse on the counter and removed her little Nikon. She could remember when a camera like this would have cost her a week's salary. Now they practically gave them away in boxes of breakfast cereal.

All right. She'd been putting it off but the moment was here. She crossed the living room again and stood at the bedroom doorway. She remembered the first time she'd crossed that threshold with Carter. It wasn't the first time they'd been to bed together. That had been at her place. In the very bed where she'd found his body.

She flashed back on that moment. Had she even looked at his face? He'd been lying on his back, wearing a pair of her panties and almost wearing one of her bras. She could see the knife sticking out of his chest, could remember exactly what it had felt like, grasping the handle, feeling the slippery blood, tugging at it until she'd got it out of his chest.

But had she even seen his face? Were his eyes open or closed? Did he have a look of surprise, or had he been in agony when he died?

She felt herself getting dizzy.

She half-leaned, half-fell against the bedroom door. It swung open and she staggered into the room. She could smell something in the air. A faint odor of cigar smoke, and a cheap, young-girl perfume mixed with harsh female musk.

She felt her knees turning to jelly as she stumbled toward the bed. This was impossible. Impossible. Another comforter, another shape, another tent.

This couldn't be real. This was some kind of mad, psychotic flashback.

She leaned against the bed, her knees against the side of the bed, the Nikon in her left hand; with her right hand she pulled back the comforter.

Another body. Another kitchen knife. Another pair of red panties. Another lacy red brassiere.

Marianne the bimbo.

Her head was whirling, blackness descending over her, her ears ringing. She felt herself falling into a bottomless pit. She'd never fainted in her life and now she had a fleeting moment of self-awareness in which she thought, *this is what fainting is.*

She thought, it was like passing out drunk.

Just one look at you, my heart grows tipsy in me.

Warm flesh against her face. She opened her eyes, let out a brief scream, pushed against, against what? Against Marianne the bimbo? Flesh still warm but not like a living person. And her face was wet; she touched her cheek, slippery, brought her hand away, red.

She tried to stand up, found herself on her knees beside the bed, unable to rise.

She heard a door open and turned. The bathroom door. Carter's bathroom. For a crazed moment she remembered that she'd kept a toothbrush there to use when she stayed over with Carter.

You and you alone bring out the gypsy in me.

He was standing in the doorway. Not Carter. Who the hell was he? Hound's tooth jacket. Thick glasses. Bifocal line. The loser from Mildred's.

For a few seconds they stared at each other, Dorothy and the hapless pick-up artist, a frozen tableau. She remembered his newspaper. It was *The Detroit Free Press.* If Carter wouldn't go to Detroit, then Detroit would come to Carter.

He lunged for the bed, reached for the knife sticking out of Marianne the bimbo. Dorothy hit the button on the Nikon and the little camera flashed in the man's face. He threw his hands up and tumbled backwards across the bed. Dorothy whirled and ran for the doorway, stumbled across the living room.

Before she could reach the doorway the door swung open and two figures entered.

She recognized them.

Behind her she heard an incoherent male sound, something between a grunt and a roar. She tried to turn and see who was coming but her momentum made her tumble over backwards. She landed on her rump, the Nikon still clutched against her shoulder.

The man in the hound's tooth jacket had a bloody knife in his hand and he was coming at her. She fired the camera at him again, heard a crash from behind her, saw a startled look on the man's face, heard another crash and saw red spots appearing on his jacket. She snapped another frame and watched him tumble to the carpet and lie still.

She felt strong hands pulling her to her feet, blinked and saw Officer Galloway. He lifted her and she clung to him. She turned her face and saw Jackie McKibbon bending over the man in the hound's tooth jacket. She kicked the kitchen knife away, put a couple of fingers on the side of his neck and nodded.

Dorothy leaned away from Galloway. "I'm okay. I'm okay."

Galloway muscled her to the nearby sofa and lowered her as if she were a child. She aimed the Nikon and snapped another exposure of the man in the hound's tooth jacket.

Now Galloway rumbled away, into the bedroom. A minute later he was back. Jackie McKibbon was doing something with the body on the carpet and Dorothy took another picture. Galloway signaled to Jackie McKibbon and she followed him into the bedroom. A minute later she was back in the living room, sitting with Dorothy.

Now Galloway came walking out of the bedroom shaking his head.

Dorothy looked at the two cops, Galloway and McKibbon. "How did you know?"

"We didn't, we were just keeping an eye on you, Miss Doe. We did have an eye on Timmy Stander, though."

Dorothy frowned, puzzled.

"Him." Jackie McKibbon indicated the man on the floor.

"But—why? What's the connection?"

"Hanson was buying counterfeit twenties in Detroit, paying for them with good cash and bringing the queer bills back to Chicago. The printing plant is in Windsor. They print U.S. phony there and smuggle it into Detroit for distribution."

"I don't get it. Why would anybody swap good money for counterfeit?"

McKibbon laughed. "It wasn't one for one. Going rate for queer bucks is something like twenty per cent of face value. Anyway"— she ran her fingers through her hair—"anyway, Hanson must have run some kind of double-cross on his customers. I heard of one of these double-crosses where a bad guy tried to buy counterfeit money with counterfeit money. He even got away with it for a little while. Eventually he wound up in Lake Michigan. Whatever Hanson was up to, the Detroit people sent Stander to straighten him out."

Dorothy was starting to get her bearings again. She peered at the man lying on the floor. "He doesn't look like an enforcer."

"No." Jackie McKibbon nodded. "No fedora, no pencil moustache, no pinstripe suit, right? That's just the point, Dorothy."

She touched Dorothy's hand. "This is some building. Shots fired and nobody says boo. We'll have to call this in, get people up here."

Dorothy said, "He must have stolen my bra and panties as a gift for her. I never even missed them. He was crazy about red lace, red lace bras and panties. I had a drawer full of them. I never even missed them."

Jackie McKibbon smiled. "They are nice."

"They came from Marshall Fields," Dorothy told her. She stood up and made her way back to the bedroom. McKibbon tagged along, watching Dorothy's every move.

She stood over the dresser where she sometimes kept a few changes of clothing, a convenience for those times she'd stayed over with Hanson. She slid the drawer open. It was filled with red lacy underthings. She reached in and picked up a couple of sets of undies.

From behind her she heard McKibbon's hissed exclamation. She saw McKibbon reach past her and pull more underwear aside, exposing the carefully packaged sheaves of twenty-dollar bills.

Richard Lupoff has written sixty volumes of fantasy, mystery, science fiction, horror, and mainstream fiction. His recent books include the collections *Killer's Dozen*, *Quintet: the Cases of Chase and Delacroix*, *Before 12:01 and After*, *The Universal Holmes*, and *Terrors, Visions, and Dreams*. His nine-volume mystery series involving Hobart Lindsey and Marvia Plum was reissued by Wildside Press in 2013.

HANGIN' WITH IRON MIKE

by Stan Trybulski

1

I had just finished playing hoops and was walking off the asphalt court when Nia came running down the street toward me. Even though she was still up the block I could hear her screaming and crying.

"They killed Arnold," she sobbed, running into my arms and holding me.

"Who?"

"That big thug Iraq! Him and his crew."

Nia was my little sister, at thirteen, two years younger than me, and Arnold was our pet pigeon. We didn't live in the projects but in a three-story building that was better than a tenement. It had clean apartments and the front door had good locks. We could even use the roof and Ma let me raise a pigeon up there. I let Nia name him. She called him Arnold. I didn't like the name too much but hey, Nia's my little sister and has the prettiest smile in Brooklyn so the bird was named Arnold.

2

When I saw the bird lying on the tar paper roof, its neck all twisted and its tiny eyes looking up at nothing I wanted to cry too. But I just stared blankly at the bird. Iraq and two of his buddies were there laughing at the bird and at me. They didn't care about front door locks; they had scaled the backyard fence and climbed up the fire escape.

"I killed your bird, punk," Iraq said. "Want to fight me?"

They call him Iraq because that's where he says his father was killed while in the Army. I know the true story; the one where Iraq's mother, pregnant with him, called the cops after her baby-daddy broke her arm. She had him arrested but he booked before the court date and nobody has seen him since. At least that's what Ma told me when I asked her about it.

Iraq was a year older than me and heavier and training to become a boxer. I didn't want to fight him, I wanted to kill him and if I had a nine of my own or even a pipe I would have but I knew that at fifteen I could be tried as an adult for murder and even if I was tried as a juvenile they could send me to Spofford and then to Coxsackie until I was twenty-one. That was six years and who would protect Nia while I was gone? So I just kept staring at the bird and saying nothing.

"See you around, sweet thing," Iraq said to Nia, rubbing his hand along her arm as he walked by. I wanted to kill him more than ever but I still kept staring at Arnold.

After Iraq and his crew swaggered off, I put my arm around Nia and wiped her tears and promised we would get another pigeon and that she could name that one too.

We buried Arnold in the vacant lot next door but I didn't bury my hate.

3

I used my allowance to buy another pigeon and some gorilla glue. I gave the pigeon to Nia as a birthday present. I told her that it was all hers and she would have to feed and care for it and she cried and hugged me.

I paid a homeless man five cents each for some beer bottles he had taken from a street corner trash basket and I took them up to the roof of our building. I put a towel on the tar paper and broke the bottles. Then I took the sharpest, most jagged pieces I could find and used the gorilla glue to paste them on the parapet around the top of the fire escape. The glass was dark brown like the brick of the parapet and you couldn't really see it. I was hoping Iraq and his crew would come back but they never did. That was okay I decided because I knew I would find another way.

4

I went down to the precinct stationhouse. Not to file a complaint against Iraq for killing my bird. I had heard that the Police Athletic League had a boxing program and I wanted to join. The administrative aide at the desk told me it was on Pennsylvania Avenue in Brownsville and told me to ask for Detective McDermott. I went there straight away.

I told McDermott that there was this kid named Iraq in my school who was supposed to be a pretty boxer and that I wanted to learn to box like him. McDermott said that Iraq was a good boxer and that he would be fighting in the Golden Gloves next year, but that he didn't train with the PAL. I said I didn't care; I wanted to learn enough to fight in the Golden Gloves too. He said he would teach me how to fight but the rest, the discipline and the heart I had to have. I just nodded and thought of Arnold.

The detective called boxing the sweet science and said I had to study it just like I was in school. I never was much good in school, Nia was the smart one in the family, and we knew she was going to college, going somewhere big in life. No one had ever said that about me. But I listened and I studied. McDermott taught me how to jab and throw a hook and a straight right; showed me how I needed to stick and move.

"This isn't the street," he said. "You're going to meet guys in the ring that are faster than you and hit harder. You won't be able to use a bat or knife or a gun. You won't be able to block all their punches."

So he taught me how to move from side to side, to slip punches and counter, how to roll my head and body away when I was hit to lessen the impact. And all the time he had me moving around the ring, running, skipping rope, building up my wind. I could have taken the subway to the PAL gym but I ran there and back every day instead.

5

When I turned sixteen I got a job in the supermarket. I gave Ma money every week and saved the rest. This was the same year I saw Mike Tyson fight for the first time. Everybody in Brooklyn knew Iron Mike and his rep but us kids were too young to have ever have seen him fight live in the ring. Then they started showing his greatest knockouts on television and I watched them all. He was packing C-4 in both hands. I wanted to be just like him and take Iraq out but I knew that I had to have a special plan, a special program beyond the PAL gym.

As soon as I had saved enough, I bought a heavy bag, a set of free weights and a bench and set them up in the basement. Ma didn't mind, she was happy to see me not watching TV all night long. I knew I had to work hard. Iraq had stopped Nia on the street one day and told her how good she looked and that she about ready for her first man and that she should start hanging with him. She spit in his face and moved back just as he tried to slap her.

He wiped the spit off his face and laughed an evil laugh. "Bitch, the next time I see you, you'll do the wiping," he warned her. Nia came home crying and said she was scared of him but I told her not worry, just stay out of his way for a while and I'll take care of everything.

I bought a poster of Iron Mike and put it up on the basement wall so I could always see his scowl when I worked out. I decided that if boxing was a science like McDermott said then this was my own personal lab. So after working out at the PAL gym, I would go home and watch DVD's of Iron Mike. Afterwards, I would go down in the basement and throw left hooks at the heavy bags, imagining where Iraq's liver and temple and jaw were. One day while watching a sports show on ESPN, I saw an old interview of Iron Mike where he said he was going to drive his opponent's nose bone up into his brain. I smiled.

6

I asked Nia where I could buy some books and she took me to the Barnes & Noble store downtown on Court Street. It was cool inside and they had a Starbucks café upstairs. So I let Nia get some books and bought her an iced lemonade drink and left her at a little round table with a high bar-type chair in the café while I searched for what I needed. I didn't know my way around the store so I asked a clerk and he sent me to the sports section. There was a whole collection of books about martial arts and I looked through them until I found the one I wanted. It described in detail how to break someone's nose with a punch and then drive the broken bone up into the skull by using the heel of your hand. I didn't even have to read it because there was a series of photos that showed me exactly what to do. I studied them very carefully.

When I came back to the café Nia was still reading at the little round table where I had left her. Even with her long kid braids and her thin legs dangling down from the high stool, she looked grown up. I was so proud of her that I wished I could have taken a picture for Ma to keep.

7

As soon as we got home Nia went to her room to do her homework and I went down to the basement and wrapped my hands and hung out with Iron Mike. I saw the photos from the martial arts books in my mind and practiced the punches over and over again. First the left hook to the liver—my money punch—and then what the book said. I swear that once when I looked up at the poster of Iron Mike, he wasn't scowling, he was smiling. I smiled back.

The Golden Gloves is almost as good as the pros, at least if you make it to the finals. Then you get to fight in the Garden. By the time the tournament rolled around, McDermott said I was ready and he was right. I was going to fight as a novice just like Iraq and I had put on enough pounds and muscle so that we would be in the same weight class. He wasn't planning on losing and neither was I, so sooner or later we would meet up. I hooked and jabbed my way to the final and Iraq slugged his way to the top as well. McDermott told me I would have to punch more, use my right hand behind my jab and after the left hook if I wanted to beat Iraq.

I just nodded my head and said I won't let you down. He smiled, never knowing that I was really speaking to Nia.

8

I looked over the ropes at Iraq bouncing down the aisle like he was a champ and I smiled. When he got in the ring he smirked at me. "I'm going break your neck just like I did to your pigeon, punk."

I just kept smiling.

The fight only lasted one round. I came out jabbing like I always do but Iraq was so damn street anxious to hurt me that he threw a wild right. I slipped it easily and ripped a vicious left hook to his liver. He half bent over, almost paralyzed, and I threw my right and connected. It wasn't the straight right to the jaw that McDermott had taught me to throw after the hook, it was the downward chopping punch I learned from the martial arts book and it landed on the bridge of Iraq's nose and right between the eyes. Even with the boxing glove covering my fist, the side of my hand was like a steel bar. I could hear Iraq's nose bone splinter. I clinched and spun Iraq so the ref was behind him and didn't have a clear view. I looked right into Iraq's eyes and smiled. Then I rammed the heel of my hand up against the tip of his nose, sending the shards of broken bone deep into his brain. He shuddered and keeled over.

I was happy. After tonight Iraq would never bother Nia again. No one would. They can't send you upstate for killing a kid in the ring, can they?

✗

Stan Trybulski, who wrote *One Trick Pony* and other crime novels, was a Brooklyn felony trial prosecutor before he went into private practice. Before he entered the legal profession, he was a newspaper reporter, college administrator, and bartender (not all at the same time). He says that he now divides his time between France and "two acres of Connecticut tranquility."

INSPECTOR ROMFORD'S GREATEST CASES

by John Grant

It was Romford's 65th birthday, and the day of his retirement from the Yard. He and a few select colleagues—fellow senior officers plus Romford's longtime secretary Miss Rutherford—conducted the farewell party at lunchtime at their usual pub, the Spoon & Lobster, and of course it had gone on longer than it should. Miss Rutherford openly wept on his shoulder; when she looked as if she might be sick—and hadn't she had six glasses of Ruby Red port, no less?—he'd phoned for a taxi to take her home. Now he was here on his own in his office, boxing up the last of his personal possessions. Tonight would be the last time he'd finish his working day by taking the 7:45 from Waterloo to the little village of Cadaver-in-the-Offing, where Mrs. Romford would have his slippers warmed and ready for him.

The carton was almost full. There was only one more important item to pack, and then he'd be on his way.

He slid open a deep side-drawer of his desk, then pulled it with a hard tug so that it came off its runners. Reaching into the dark space behind, he fished out a large black notebook. In a fit of self-indulgence a few years ago, he'd stuck a label on the front of the notebook that read, in his own crisply inked block capitals:

INSPECTOR ROMFORD'S GREATEST CASES

The elderly detective read the label once, twice, and felt the memories flooding back. He tussled the drawer back onto its tracks and flopped into the chair behind his desk, pulling the notebook towards him.

The writing on the earliest page had faded from black to a sort of rusty, streaked brown, but was still legible enough.

BATTLEY, Martin, sentenced to life imprisonment on 3 July 1981 at Teesside Crown Court on 14 counts of rape and murder committed over a three-year period in...

Romford sighed. That had been his first big success, the one that brought him to the attention of the Yard. Battley was still alive in prison, still—like so many of them—swearing vengeance against Romford for banging him up.

Romford ran his eyes over the pages, his gaze resting only on the highlights. It was interesting to watch how the handwriting became more mature with each new entry.

GUBBINS, Theodore, sentenced to life imprisonment on 14 December 1986 at Colchester Crown Court on 11 counts of murder by strangulation between 1981 and...

DINBROODY, Albert John, sentenced to life imprisonment after pleading guilty on 29 February 1996 at the Old Bailey on 26 counts of sexual molestation and murder...

That had been the big one. He'd not just nailed the profoundly slow-witted Dinbroody, he'd actually persuaded the simpleton to confess. There had been features about Scotland Yard's new star in the newspapers and magazines for weeks and months afterwards. He'd gone from being just plain old Chief Inspector Romford to "Romford of the Yard"—a household name like those great cops before him: Fabian, Stryker, Gideon...

He closed the notebook and tossed it into the carton.

A life in crime. Of course, it wasn't the complete account by any means. That was contained in his full-scale autobiography, which would take the form of the diary he'd been secretly dictating over the years onto cassette tapes that he stored in a secret box in the potting shed. After Romford's death, his solicitor would open the letter he'd left giving instructions as to where the tapes were, and what to do with them. The resulting book could hardly fail to be a sensation.

Romford was nationally renowned already. His retirement would make the national TV and radio news tonight.

But this was as nothing compared to how brightly his posthumous fame would shine.

✗   ✗   ✗   ✗

As the little suburban train clattered along between stations, Romford lost himself in thought.

He fondled the pipe in his jacket pocket, longing for the days before smoking was banned on trains.

In retrospect, it was so strange that none of his colleagues had ever noticed the similarity in *modus operandi* of the men Romford had succeeded in putting away as serial killers—Battley, Gubbins, Dinbroody and the others. The strangled bodies had always been found in a remote tract of forest, fully dressed and with an ivory chess piece lodged between their teeth. They'd all been rendered unconscious using ether before being molested and strangled. Most obvious of all, their forenames ran in order from A to Z and then starting again at A, the alphabetical sequence being uninterrupted between one supposed perpetrator and the next.

No one had thought to take a second look at the living legend of British policing who nabbed the men.

And no one had ever uncovered Romford's secret motto: *You can't get to the top of the promotional heap without breaking a few eggs.*

But they'd surely pay heed when, after his death, his autobiography was typed up and published, complete with details of the murders that had never been released to the public, not even during the various trials.

Romford wasn't sure he believed in the afterlife, but he hoped that somehow he'd be able to watch everyone's faces when they learned the truth…

✗   ✗   ✗   ✗

Sure enough, when he got home to Blossom Cottage he found that Mrs. Romford had warmed his slippers and put a schooner of sweet sherry on the low table beside his armchair in front of the fire. In her own slippers, which were of the carpet variety, she plodded around putting the final touches to their celebratory dinner: Yorkshire pudding with all the trimmings followed by a nice Bird's Eye trifle, and everything washed down with a glass or two of room-temperature Sauternes.

This banquet consumed, they returned to the fireside.

Mrs. Romford's eyes could not often be said to dance—the most they ordinarily managed was a sort of ungainly shuffle—but they were dancing tonight.

"You may be wondering about your birthday present," she said coyly.

"I already have the best birthday present I could ever wish for," her husband responded gallantly. "You, my love!"

Her chin dimpled. "You saucy rogue. But I've got you *another* gift, one that I know you'll like. You know that little strongbox you keep in the potting shed that you think I don't know about..."

Romford sat bolt upright, no mean feat what with all the sherry and the Yorkshire pud and the trifle and, oh God, the Sauternes.

"I've sent all your tapes off to a transcription service in London with a nice fat check to cover the expense..."

She paused, then added, "Do I need to call the doctor, my dear?"

✗

John Grant is author of over sixty books. Among his nonfiction works have been *The Encyclopedia of Walt Disney's Animated Characters* (three editions), *The Encyclopedia of Fantasy* (with John Clute), and a series of books about false belief and manipulation in science: *Discarded Science, Corrupted Science, Bogus Science*, and most recently *Denying Science*. For his nonfiction he has received the Hugo Award (twice), the World Fantasy Award, and various others. Under a different name he has received a Chesley Award and a World Fantasy Award nomination for his work editing the fantasy artbook imprint Paper Tiger. His most recently completed book is the monumental *A Comprehensive Encyclopedia of Film Noir*, which he proudly boasts is longer than the Old Testament; it was released in the fall of 2013. His most recent fictions are two stand-alone novellas published by PS Publishing: the Ed McBain homage *The City in These Pages* and the noir-tinged literary mystery/fantasy *The Lonely Hunter*.

THE LAST SONG

by Dianne Neral Ell

On that first Tuesday in August, Amanda Haines sped east along Route 27 toward Bridgehampton, Long Island. It was the beginning of a three week hiatus, or vacation as she preferred to think of it—a time between her old case load with the FBI in Washington D.C. and her new assignment with the Paris, France, office. For three weeks there would be nothing but solitude on her agenda. No new cases, cold cases, anything having to do with crime investigation. Three wonderful empty weeks where the most complicated decision she'd make was whether to have white wine or a vodka and tonic, take a walk before breakfast or swim in the pool.

As she came to the light at Ocean Drive, her cell phone rang. The screen showed it was her cousin Gil Haines, a lawyer and a member of Southampton's oldest law firm.

"Hey there," she said.

"Where are you?"

"Waiting for the light to change at Ocean. I'll be at the house in five."

"Amanda, I'm sorry. I know you're starting your first real vacation in a long time, but I got a call from George Simmons this morning. Remember him? You know him best as Will Peterson's attorney. He wants to talk to you. I put him off, but after the third call I told him you'd be at the house this afternoon and to try you there. I didn't give him your cell number. But when you get to the house you may find him on the front porch."

Amanda could feel all the good spirits taking flight from her body. "What does he want?"

"Don't know. Asked. Wouldn't say. Just wanted to warn you. Oh, and Mark Ashford is looking for you. Didn't give him the number either. Big time on Saturday night. Can't believe it's been twenty-five years."

"I know. There were signs all along twenty-seven for the concert. And of course the radio stations are anchored on their music.

Wonder where they'd be now if you hadn't come up with the name 'Mark Ashford and the Surfriders'."

"They'd still be sitting on the front porch." He laughed. "Let me know what's up with Simmons."

Turning south at the light, Amanda rode past century-old estates. At Surfside Drive, the last street before the ocean, she turned left and four houses down made another left into the Haines family summer home driveway. She parked her dark gray rental around back of the rambling two-story brown shingle structure with its new turquoise trim and entered through the back door dragging her two stuffed suitcases behind her.

She pulled the suitcases down the main hall with its highly polished hardwood floors and up the stairs to the room she had always loved—front room with a view—of Aunt Ellen's rose bushes, the dunes and the ocean.

Amanda put one suitcase in the closet and the other on the bed. Fifteen years of FBI training had her opening her laptop and sending an email to the office that she had arrived in Bridgehampton.

In the far corner of the room, leaning against the wall, was a framed, signed, twenty-fifth anniversary edition poster of Mark Ashford and the Surfriders tagged for Ellen's art gallery. Ellen Haines, her mother's youngest sister, lived in the house nearly year round. An excellent artist, she was also part owner of a Southampton art gallery, and one of the local museums.

As Gil mentioned, it was on their front porch, that night in August so long ago, that the Surfriders were born. Until then, they were a summer band, casually linked through music and membership in the Bridgehampton Tennis Club, who called themselves the Dropouts. She could still see that night—where everyone sat, what they were wearing, what they were drinking. And always, the history making moment when Sara Ragland ran up the porch steps, out of breath, talking about a band competition with the winner opening for Bon Jovi in two weeks at the Westbury. They decided to compete. The Dropouts became Mark Ashford and the Surfriders. And twenty-five years later they were still riding the top of the charts.

There were about a dozen people on the porch that night. One of whom was Will Peterson, who went on to become one of the most popular composers of music for movies and Broadway. He wrote many of the early Surfrider songs. Will died a decade ago in Southampton from a fall on his yacht. She hoped Simmons' call wasn't about Will.

As she closed the suitcase, Louis jumped up on the bed. He sat looking expectantly at her.

"I was wondering where you were," she said to the large, orange tabby. She leaned over and kissed his forehead. Then gave him a hug. He nuzzled his nose against her cheek then jumped down.

"That was it?" she laughed as she called after him. "It's been a year and that's the best greeting you can give me?"

As she looked after Louis, the phone rang.

It was George Simmons. He apologized for the interruption then he asked if she could come to his office this afternoon. He knew it was late but the matter was urgent. Knowing there'd be no peace unless she did, Amanda agreed to be there within the half hour. She took a comb to her shoulder-length blond hair, added some liner to her blue eyes, refreshed her lipstick, and headed downstairs to get her car.

⚹   ⚹   ⚹   ⚹

Twenty minutes later she arrived at the Simmons and Hollis law firm in Southampton. One step into the conference room told her she was right. This was about Will Peterson. Surrounding George Simmons was Will's sister Terra Peterson, an old summer buddy, now famous star of stage and screen, and Clint Barnsworth, the consulting medical examiner still looking as the last time she saw him except his dark, curling hair now had streaks of gray. There had been a time when she thought she and Barnsworth could have been more than a nine-to-five investigative team. After the case they worked together in Miami ended, there were tries at getting together. But the timing was never on their side. Was this the to-morrow they promised themselves five years ago?

"What brings us together?" Amanda asked, joining them at the table. She gave Terra a hug, and shook hands with Simmons, then with Clint until he took the move and kissed her on the cheek.

"I couldn't believe it when George said you were the FBI agent joining our small task force," Clint said.

"Task force. What task force? I'm here on vacation."

No one paid attention to the word 'vacation.'

"This is why we're together. It was sent to Terra and me." As they sat down Simmons handed Amanda a copy of a typed sheet of paper. It stated *'It was time Will Peterson's killer was brought to justice. Crime scene photos should tell the tale.'*

"Will's killer? Not an accident?" She looked at Barnsworth.

"The letter's right," he answered.

Amanda felt her limbs going weak. "After ten years someone decides to send this. Did it come to the office?" She looked at Simmons.

He nodded.

"Then everyone here knows about it?" Amanda asked.

"As does almost everyone on the police force," Barnsworth added. "We had to go through them for Will's case files. Ten-year-old solved cases are kept in the same warehouse as the Lost Ark. It took some doing but we got it."

"What was in the files?" Amanda asked. "There was no investigation. He died from a fall."

"Police report and photographs," Barnsworth said. "Take a look at this. The second is a blow-up of the first."

The photograph he handed her showed the back of Will Peterson's head. Plainly, someone had taken a hard object and bashed it in just behind his right ear. Clint had enlarged the photo to where she could see a partial imprint of the murder weapon in the skull.

"How did this get overlooked?" she asked.

"The police were not the first on the scene," Simmons said. "Paramedics arrived after a 911 call. And they moved the body to see if he was still alive. It was over an hour before the police got there. A couple of rookies showed up and took photos. And the assistant M.E. never made it. Will was placed in an ambulance and taken to the hospital."

"He was on his back… still…" Amanda shook her head. The pain of lost opportunity shot through her. She should have been on this. Ten years is a long time in which to try and find Will's killer.

Terra asked for the photos. She looked at the one of Will after he landed. "It doesn't look like he tried to break the fall."

"His arms are to his side," Barnsworth said. "It means he was already dead or at least unconscious as he fell. The photos also show that the stairwell walls had no blood smears. No doubt it was murder."

"We'd like to keep the investigation as close to the chest as possible." Simmons looked at Terra then at Amanda. "Besides being an FBI agent, you knew Will. I know you're on vacation, but can you help?"

For a chance to work with Barnsworth again. To do something she should have done ten years ago, she said 'yes.' But she wouldn't call the office until she had a chance to see what kind of success she had reconstructing the past. "I should know within a day or two if I can piece together enough evidence to solve this."

"I need to return to Queens tonight to finish up a case," Barnsworth said. "I'll be back by Friday. This should keep you going in the meantime." He slid an envelope across the table to Amanda. "Photos, my report, and some extraneous information you might need along with how to reach me at all times."

Amanda gave out a business card to all with her new cell number on it.

As the group broke up, Terra said to Amanda, "Let's get together while you're here. And if you need me for anything," she took a card from her pocket, "call me on this number." She didn't offer it to Simmons or Barnsworth. Then she was gone.

The three walked downstairs to the sidewalk. Barnsworth asked Amanda to call him in the morning and let him know how she would proceed. Then he left leaving Amanda and George Simmons alone.

"Drink?" Simmons asked.

"Why not."

✗   ✗   ✗   ✗

"What happened to the rest of Will's items? From the boat? From the house?" she asked after they found seats at the bar of a busy after-work establishment.

"There's an inventory from the boat inside that envelope Clint gave you," he said. "As for the house, there wasn't much. I shipped his music to Los Angeles. Clothes went to charity. Sculptures, paintings were handled by Christies in New York. There's an inventory and photos of their items inside Barnsworth's envelope.

The man is thorough. And a local company came in to handle the sale of the furniture. Terra was there as was Mallory, Will's friend. Talk to her."

"I will."

"I always meant to tell you how sorry I was about your car accident."

Amanda looked down at her left hand. "The French doctors repaired it beautifully. But it couldn't take the strain of being a touring concert pianist so I had to find another occupation. I was lucky. I was famous enough to get booked into embassy events. 'An evening with Amanda Haines at the American Embassy in Paris.' That kind of thing. When I was slated for the Russian Embassy, a friend from the FBI Paris office asked me to do a favor. Kind of undercover. I loved it. Was invited to join and never looked back."

"So what division of the FBI are you in?"

"White collar crime. Art theft division."

For just a moment Simmons' smile faltered. Then he regained it. "Interesting."

✗　✗　✗　✗

It was after seven by the time she made it back to the house. Just enough light remained for her walk. She gave Louis his dinner as well as a few ounces of meatloaf which he devoured immediately and left some dry food for Sami. She changed into beach clothes, removed her sandals and armed with a Pinot Grigio in one hand, camera in the other, and a flashlight in her pants pocket, she headed across the dunes to the beach and west along the shoreline into the setting sun.

The beach was a straight line for a while, then it widened as it began to curve toward the Bridgehampton Surf and Tennis Club. She had already walked about fifteen minutes and the Club was as far as she intended to go. It would be dusk by the time she reached it.

She flipped on her camera and stopped to snap a few photos. As she paused, the edge of the incoming tide swirled about her bare feet. The coldness of the water made her jump, and she moved a few feet inward from the water's edge to where the sand still held the warmth of the sun. At that moment, she heard what sounded like a bee cutting the air just to the left of where she had stood. A bullet. Someone was shooting at her. She dropped to the sand wishing she had brought her gun.

She remained inert for a few more moments. When no more bees buzzed by, she scooted across the sand to the nearest dune. Judging from where she had stood, a straight line would put the shooter on a dune to the east of her.

In the distance, she heard the sound of a motorcycle gunning its engine. In a moment it was gone leaving only the residue of waves washing upon the beach.

Crawling to the top of the dune, she looked around. Houses were far apart. Dune grass and various types of sand shrubs separated her from the road. Whoever it was had left. She pulled out her flashlight and stepped carefully, looking for the place the shooter might have stood. In the glow she found shoe prints. Not the entire shoe but enough to take a photo. Holding the flashlight in her teeth, she shot off a few. The prints had to belong to the shooter. If they had been there earlier, the evening breeze would have dusted them with a layer of sand.

Someone followed her and waited. From the terrain, probably used a rifle with a suppressor. Who would have one of those things except for the police? And possibly cousin Gil. No coincidences. Therefore, it had to do with the Will Peterson case.

She looked down the long stretch of beach where night was rapidly settling in. Time to return to the house. Welcome back Amanda Lee Haines.

✗   ✗   ✗   ✗

The late morning air had the oppressive heat of August as Amanda got out of her car in front of Canfield Shoes. She went in hoping to find Emory, the owner who was a friend of her father's. He was there and was happy to help. She showed him the photos taken at the dunes.

"It's a designer shoe. But that's all I know right now. Give me your number. I'll call you when I have something. Might not be until late tomorrow. How's your parents?"

"Hong Kong."

"Still doing those government gigs?"

"They'll be here in October."

"I'll see them then."

Amanda handed him a card with her cell phone number on it.

✗   ✗   ✗   ✗

Her next stop was the storage facility where she was meeting George Simmons. Will's death occurred on the Friday of the second week of September. Re-creating the week he died was the place to start. Earlier this morning she went online and found articles in local newspapers and magazines that provided a backdrop for that time in September. But she needed Will's perspective for the foreground. That would only come from his personal items.

The two-story storage facility on Hill Street resembled a hotel on the outside. The interior was divided into spaces that looked like large offices complete with floor to ceiling storage cabinets, a desk and table. Will's items were piled in three boxes. Not much of it mattered except for his appointment book, a music journal, and another notebook for personal ramblings.

Amanda put them in a beach bag. "This will give me a start," she said.

"If you want to get back in here let me know," Simmons said.

She waited until he walked away then she headed for her car. Most of her work would center around Southampton. It made sense to find a space to work here rather than sitting in her car or traveling back to the house. Picking up lunch, she made sure she wasn't followed, then checked into a motel two blocks away. The room had adequate space along with two sofas, a desk and a large dining table. And no one looking over her shoulder or asking questions.

The information in the appointment book was fairly readable. That week Will met with Mark Ashford, a woman named Lina Walsh, and Mallory Griffin. She grazed through the music diary and the third notebook in which he had written his thoughts on meetings and projects. That would need more time to review.

Mark Ashford was her favorite suspect. He carried an anger that could have erupted in murder over Will reneging on a music deal. Songs promised but never delivered. While that happened long before Will's death it could be a matter, as the French say, of revenge being a dish best served cold. Only one way to know. She punched in the last number she had for him. He answered.

After all the 'how are yous' and was she coming to the concert, she invited him to dinner tonight. He agreed and said he'd bring the band and some steaks. He already knew about Will's investigation.

"Is interrogation part of the entertainment?" he asked jokingly.

"I'll be talking to anyone who can tell me something."

"At least I have an alibi. See you at six thirty."

She called her aunt and cousin and left messages about the extras for dinner, then she called Barnsworth to tell him about someone using her for target practice. "I got a photo of a shoe print from the sand dune. May or may not lead to something. I'll know tomorrow."

"Unfortunately, there was no discreet way to get Will's case files," he said. "Add to that the poor handling of the letter at the law firm. Maybe the whole town knows."

"Mark Ashford, my number one suspect, who's coming to dinner tonight, knew about the investigation. The power of word of mouth."

"But how many knew you'd be working on it?" he pointed out. "I'll look at gun registrations. Not sure we'll find the sniper that way but it's a start. And refrain from beach walks until I get there."

Amanda agreed. She checked her watch. There was enough time to visit the scene of the crime. The house Will owned back then was on water near the end of a small peninsula. The southern tip of the sliver of land was a sanctuary and across the inlet was an Indian Reservation. The house was pretty isolated.

She parked in the sanctuary's small visitor parking area. Various paths had been cut through the salt scrub to the water. Amanda took one that paralleled the house and within five minutes reached the shoreline where she had a good view of the house and the dock where a large, maybe sixty-foot power boat was anchored.

The route from the house across the lawn to the dock, then down the long dock to the boat was the same now as it was ten years ago. One could not reach the boat without being seen. Therefore, Will knew the person who killed him.

⚹　⚹　⚹　⚹

Ellen was in the kitchen when Amanda returned at four thirty. Louis and the second cat Sami were curled up on chairs on the back porch. Her aunt looked good. She was the prettiest and youngest of her mother's sisters. Medium height, graceful, with blond hair cut short that always looked great regardless of the weather. In all her years, it probably never saw an ounce of hair spray. She was ten years beyond Amanda's forty-two.

Cousin Gil arrived a little after five. With well-cut blondish brown hair and a trim, muscular build, he usually maintained a *Gentleman's Quarterly* appearance. Always a kind of adventurer, he served in the Gulf Wars, then in Intelligence in Afghanistan. When he wasn't at the law firm, he could be found on the links or at the helm of his fifty-five foot Hatteras moored in Sag Harbor.

Around six thirty, Amanda heard the cars of Mark and the band pull into the driveway. Mark was tall, maybe six-two, and except for a few lines they were all getting around the eyes and mouth, he was still a good looking man with his down-to-the-collar head of hair and a powerful stage presence.

As the evening progressed, Amanda tried to imagine Gil, Mark, and even Ellen traipsing along the dunes at twilight looking for the best place to take a shot at her. It seemed inconceivable it was one of them. Then again, they were all athletic enough to have done it.

When the dinner plates started to be cleared away, Mark and Amanda left the group and headed for the beach. As they sat down he said, "So the letter went to Terra and Simmons? Wonder why it didn't go to the police? Different chief now."

"Whoever sent it wanted action. The police don't answer to Terra but George does." Amanda sipped her glass of wine.

"So how was Terra?" he asked.

"Very business-like. Not emotional. Antagonistic toward George. Was wondering if she sent it. Had to be someone close to the case."

"Well, if you had me pegged as the bad guy you'll have to find someone else. That week was important for us. Our Far East tour was coming together and another album was in the works. I went to the city that day to do contracts. I called Will before I left to tell him I couldn't make our afternoon meeting but I could do dinner. He didn't answer so I left a message. Didn't hear back so I called again around two. Still didn't answer. Then, on the way back I stopped at his house. I think it was around seven, to see if he was free. Police cars surrounded the place. I went in. And Sheriff Davis, I think that was his name, told me about Will's accident.

"I mentioned Will had some papers for me. He was okay with me going into Will's office to find them. The office was a mess. Not like someone was riffling through it. Just disorganized. Besides his music, he was working on some book, and then there were maps all over the place. But sitting on top, as though he had been waiting for me to pick them up, were the songs he'd written for our band. The ones he reneged on five years before. They were stacked together. So I picked them up and left."

"What incredible luck." Amanda couldn't believe that he had an alibi for the time of the murder. How could that be possible? Her number one suspect had slipped out of her grasp. For murder. But not for theft.

⚔ ⚔ ⚔ ⚔

The smell of warm rolls and bread greeted Amanda as she entered the crowded pastry shop that Thursday morning. Mallory Griffin, the library manager, chose it as a place to meet since the library was closed on Thursdays. Since the last time she saw her a few years back, Mallory's hair was lighter and longer, which made her look younger.

"Can't believe it's almost ten years since he's been gone," Mallory said. "We were never serious but we were close. For Will, work in L.A. had been demanding that summer. September was the only time he could make it, with a promise to return at Thanksgiving. Then came the call from the woman who lived in the house on the adjacent property. She told him about people being at his house at odd hours and about this boat going in and out. It sounded strange. He asked George Simmons to look into it. I guess that wasn't enough because Will flew in in late August to investigate on his own. He stayed with me but was mainly at the woman's house… the one who called him."

"Did Will contact the police?"

Mallory paused. "I don't think so. He got copies of local maps that showed the coastline. I asked if he thought those people could be involved with one of the groups looking for buried treasure. He said he thought it could possibly be some type of criminal activity and I'd be safer if I wasn't involved."

"Does the neighbor still live in that house?"

"No. She moved some months later. Do you know Lina Walsh? The real estate agent. Maybe she knows something. She was the one who eventually sold Will's property to that British company."

"I don't remember her," but Amanda remembered the name from Will's appointment book. She paid the bill then said she'd see Mallory Friday night at Ellen's reception for the Surfriders.

On her way to the car, Amanda called Lina Walsh and arranged to see her at one thirty. Stopping at a deli, she picked up lunch then went back to the motel where she ate and reviewed Clint Barnsworth's notes. Especially the boat's inventory. Having been on it many times, she knew there was one item Will kept in his top deck cabin that he valued. A large, octagonal crystal with nautical carvings. It wasn't listed. She called Barnsworth and asked for a blowup of that section of Will's skull. She thought she could identify the murder weapon.

✗ ✗ ✗ ✗

Lina Walsh was a striking, dark-haired, well-built woman in her late forties. Her real estate office was in a gracious old building just off Job's Lane. "Will emailed me on Tuesday of the week he died," the agent said. "He wanted to sell his house as soon as possible."

"Will planned to sell the house? That's news. Why?" Amanda asked.

"Work in L.A. was demanding. And I had a client looking for such a property. There aren't many places on that south shore to anchor a large boat. The inlet that Will's house bordered on was such. I drew up the preliminary papers and dropped them at Will's house around noon on Friday. He planned to bring them over on Monday to close. The buyer was wiring in the funds and we could conclude the deal. The buyer couldn't believe his luck."

Either something happened to make Will suddenly decide to sell or Lina Walsh was lying. But why would she do that?

"Will was planning to return to the house in November for Thanksgiving. I heard this from his sister and from a friend of his. Doesn't sound like he was planning to sell."

The woman drew a deep, irritated breath. "He'd been talking about it for months. So, when he suddenly decided, I didn't think much of it."

"Since you were handling the sale, do you have any idea what became of the items in Will's house? Particularly his office," Amanda asked as she stood.

The woman's expression hardened. "I got to the house fairly early Saturday morning to make certain nothing got moved but George Simmons was already there, packing. And your aunt. I'm not sure. It's been many years."

Lina Walsh's story was total fabrication. Amanda thanked her then walked outside. At this point, a chocolate chip cone was in order. As she headed to the ice cream shop she called Terra. Getting her voice mail, she left a message about Lina and the sale of Will's house.

Stymied, she decided to the return to the motel and read through Will's journals where he must have mentioned his concerns. She spread out the maps, then opened the journal. Will arrived around the twenty-third of August. He watched the property for three nights, then he began an online search for thefts at Hampton museums and art galleries. He circled one in East Hampton.

Art thefts. Interesting. She opened the FBI's database and did the same search. There were three robberies that stood out from August to early September. A gallery in Southampton, the Museum of Modern Art in Manhattan, and the Cultural Center Museum in East Hampton. All three were major thefts. All three were still open cases.

She looked at the map and could see what Will thought he discovered. It was possible that the thieves were using his property as a base to move priceless merchandise. The items were taken from a vehicle and transferred to his house to wait for transport out of the country. Down the inlet, through the canal, and into the open ocean. So easy. Who would expect it? Or note it? Except the woman on the adjacent property.

She called Clint Barnsworth, left a message, then headed for her car.

Enough people knew she had been looking into Will's death. The sniper missed once. She might not be so lucky the second time. Had to be prepared. With a half hour before she met Ellen for dinner at a Bridgehampton restaurant, Amanda pushed the speedometer as she headed along Route 27. Two days ago she saw only leisure-enriched days ahead. She must have been reading someone else's horoscope.

The phone rang as she turned onto Ocean Drive. It was Emory Canfield. His news nearly made her plow into a potato stand near the edge of the road. He said he was not mistaken. She called Clint Barnsworth to see where he was.

"Should be there around nine or a little after," he said.

She told him about the shoes from the dunes. "They were Ferragamos, size nine. The sniper was a woman!"

Amanda never slowed until she reached the driveway. A woman. How could that be?

There was still an hour before it began to get dark. She pulled in, dashed into the house, and ran upstairs to change her clothes. She slipped into black slacks and a black long-sleeved jersey. After pinning her hair back, she added a gold necklace that softened the look of her outfit. She took her second gun out of the case then returned downstairs to check all the doors.

Louis was in the kitchen in front of empty bowls. "Thank you for keeping life in balance." She kissed him on the head. She filled both his bowls as well as Sami's, then turned on music for him. "Watch the house," she said as she ran out.

One gun was in her purse, the second in her glove compartment. She headed for dinner.

✗　✗　✗　✗

"Getting anywhere on Will's case?" Ellen asked as Amanda sat down.

The murder weapon was at the top of her mind. Ellen had given it to Will years back. She couldn't bring herself to ask about it. Instead Amanda asked about the theft at the East Hampton Cultural

Center, where Ellen was on the board. "What can you tell me about it?"

"It was horrible. The three priceless Egyptian eighteenth dynasty necklaces and two Vermeer paintings turned out to be forgeries. We don't know where or when the switch was made. Before we got them, or during the exhibition. To this day, they haven't turned up. Does this have anything to do with Will's murder?"

"I think so. It looks like Will caught onto a smuggling operation being conducted from his house when he wasn't there. His house has a unique location. It allows a large boat to come close to land where items can be loaded and unloaded and then head back out to sea without being noticed. Will's next door neighbor became suspicious of odd hour comings and goings and called him. He came back unannounced and discovered what was going on. It was just after the East Hampton theft which was in August of that year. Not sure he knew who was behind it."

"That's unbelievable." Ellen stared at her. "If the pieces did leave the country via the canal, that could be why they were never found."

Ellen looked at her watch. "We're going with some friends to hear jazz in East Hampton. It starts about nine. Why don't you come along and give yourself a break?"

✗   ✗   ✗   ✗

His gestures seemed anxious. Louis padded his front paws back and forth. Amanda wasn't familiar with the movements.

It was just before eight thirty and nearly dark. Returning from the restaurant, rather than driving around to the rear of the house, she parked out front and came through the front door. Her assailant had at least an hour to get here and find the best spot from which to take a shot. The garage offered one of the better vantage points on the property, which was why she didn't park there.

Hopefully entering from the front had thrown the sniper off balance. It would take the woman a few minutes to find another place outside to set up. Amanda turned back to Louis, who desperately wanted her attention. With one gun in her belt and the other in her hand, she followed him. He did not go to the kitchen but instead headed for the library. He walked to the French doors at the end of the room then stopped in front of the right door and pushed on it with his paw. It moved. Her assailant was in the house.

Amanda felt chills up her back as she bent down and petted him. "Good watch cat."

The room was in darkness. A slash of light from the pole light outside by the swimming pool slanted through the panes, across a section of the oriental rug, ending in the glass-enclosed display case. Her eye caught a glittering object inside the case—a large, crystal, octagonal paperweight with nautical carvings. The object Ellen had given Will so many years ago. The murder weapon.

She looked for Louis. He was gone. Her assailant was inside. She listened for a movement. A break in the air. A sound that didn't belong there. The woman was quicker than she thought. Then again, she had help.

A confrontation in the house was not the way this should end. Not inside. Too many memories that could be obliterated by a bullet. Needing to lure her assailant outside, she went out the French doors. They opened onto the patio surrounding the pool. The motion detector lights were still on. The sniper had come this way not long ago.

Keeping to the side of the house, Amanda had just reached the cover of the privacy hedge surrounding the pool when a shot buzzed by her ear.

"Damn. Where is that woman?"

Backing up against the house, she made it through an opening in the hedge and ran as fast as she could across the darkened lawn and across the road to the dunes. Another shot buzzed by her. *Let's hope third time not a charm for her*, she thought.

Reaching the first dune, she dropped to her knees and leaned against the base. Looking back to the house, she could see the porch in the glow of the living room lights, but the lawn, as it rolled to the road, faded into darkness. It was going to be hard to see anyone coming toward her.

Sitting in the sand at the base of the dune she waited. Poised. Gun forward. Suddenly there was a faint crackle to her left. Startled, she shifted her stance and began to crawl across the sand toward the sound. A shot coming from between the olive bushes nearly grazed her shoulder.

She stopped for a moment, then grabbing onto a large stone, flung it in the direction of the shot. She scrunched back into the protection of the olive plants and took aim.

Suddenly, headlights from a car cut the darkness. Her assailant lifted herself to take a shot at the approaching car.

"Hey. Yo." Amanda called out at the same time flinging another rock. The figure stopped, then to Amanda's surprise started toward her, shooting.

Amanda dropped onto the sand and raised her gun. *I'm good at moving targets,* she thought as she fired.

⚹　　⚹　　⚹　　⚹

It was the Saturday night following the Surfriders concert. Amanda and Clint sat on the front porch, he with a beer, she with a wine, being soothed by the backdrop of the rolling ocean.

"This is a nice place to come to if you don't have people shooting at you," he said. "And now that it's over, how did Lina Walsh, George Simmons, and your Aunt Ellen ever get involved in art theft?"

"It started off as a game. A Kandinsky exhibit was coming to a gallery in Southampton. Ellen had a client who wanted one of the pieces. She could oblige, and a new business was born. All three had European connections to make sales easy. But to get the art in and out of the country, they needed Will's house. All went well until Will's neighbor became curious. Reluctant to call the police, she called Will. Concerned, he came and watched his house for three nights from her property. He figured out what they were doing. And from the cars, he also knew who was involved. This included Sheriff Davis."

"Which is why Will's death never got investigated."

Amanda sighed. "Knowing the sheriff was connected to it, he decided just to show up unexpectedly. Which upset all their plans. The East Hampton exhibit had priceless articles and this time, they found a new way to protect themselves. They had them copied. Ellen did it. She found a new career. But Will told Ellen he knew what was going on and it had to stop. Further, he said if it didn't, he'd involved the FBI. And that was the end of Will."

"He had you in mind?" Clint said.

"I guess so but he never said anything. They formed a company and bought Will's house and their business continued all these years until just recently, by the slimmest of chances, Terra happened to run into someone who was with the police at the time of Will's death. It was on the set of a movie she was doing and he was there as a consultant. He said, quote: "They never caught Will's killer did they?" By the time they finished talking, Terra knew Will's death was not an accident and she hired a private investigator who could get into the storage facility where the case files were kept. One look and the investigator knew the guy was telling the truth. So she wrote the letter, sending it to herself and George, whom she suspected of being in on it."

"The case had surprises," he said. "A sniper in designer shoes. Where did Lina learn to shoot?"

"Army. Some kind of special guard unit."

"And your aunt. I'm sorry."

"I knew she was involved. She gave Will the crystal. After he was killed, she brought it home. Cleaned it off and put it in the display case along with other keepsakes."

"Cold."

"She and Will had a falling out years before then. Things didn't work out for her with Will as she hoped. The memory lingered. Unfinished business."

"Is the lesson here, beware of the friendships you make and how they end? Could come back to haunt you?"

"Especially when there's millions of dollars involved," she said.

"But you did get Mark Ashford in the end. Not for murder but for theft?"

"He got himself." Amanda smiled, and breathed deeply in satisfaction. "Will had his reasons for never turning over those songs to Mark. And Mark vowed he would get that music, over Will's dead body if necessary. And that's exactly what happened. Tuesday night at dinner he told me Will had drawn up a contract for those songs. So when Will died, he saw no reason not to take the music. Will never drew up a contract. He lied."

"And you were able to prove it?"

"Among the songs Mark took that night was the one I had worked on with Will that last morning. It was called *Perfect Strangers*. I had the score. Will faxed it to me. And the CD he emailed. Mark should never have claimed it as his own. It was the song that went on to win a Grammy, the Oscar, British, and World Music Awards. A song that catapulted Mark into the Songwriters Hall of Frame. It was the last song Will Peterson ever wrote. He needs to be remembered for it."

"Terra and the attorneys have all the evidence?"

"Yes. I'm not sure how they'll settle it but they will."

"What happens to the house and the cats?" He petted Louis who had walked out onto the porch.

"Gil's moving in. He's selling his house and getting married again. She's from a Southampton family. It's good. Louis loves him."

"We both have time before you leave for Paris." He reached for her hand.

"We can spend it here. We have the place to ourselves for two weeks. Louis and Sami need caring for. It'll be good. And after that you can come to Paris with me."

He put his drink down and stood, pulling her to stand beside him. He put his arm around her and kissed her forehead. "This is what we've been trying for for five years. It's a start."

✗

Dianne Neral Ell has written professionally for trade and consumer publications, online magazines, and websites. Her short stories have appeared in anthologies and *Sherlock Holmes Mystery Magazine. The Exhibit*, a novel of crime and suspense, is currently available at most retailers including Amazon and Barnes and Noble. She is a member of the Mystery Writers of America, the Author's Guild, and the Florida Writers Association. Her website is: www.dianneneralell.com.

SANTA AND THE SHORTSTOP

by Steve Liskow

I'm almost eight so I can read by myself, but I felt really tired and my throat was scratchy so I let Shenka read "The Night Before Christmas" to me on the couch.

"It was the night before Christmas, and all through the house…" Her accent made the words sound like scissors snipping the paper on the presents under our tree. She was from Georgia, so when I first met her I thought she'd have a southern accent, but Mom told me it was a different Georgia, over in Russia. Her real name is Natyashenka Taracova. I'm glad I don't have to write that on top of my papers at school. It would take up a whole page.

"The stockings were hung by the chimney with care…"

Her eyes flicked toward the fireplace, where the last log was still smoking.

"No stocking this year, Daniel?" She made it "stockinks." She made my name start with a "T," too. I snuggled against her and pretended my throat was really sore so I didn't have to answer. She smelled good and her sweater was soft like my blanket. She put her arm around me like I was a little kid and asked me again.

"Uh-uh." Dad said I was getting too big for Santa Claus. Mom told him I had plenty of time to grow up, but he said there's no such thing as Santa and that he and Mom put the presents under the tree and in my stocking. It made my eyes burn and my nose feel stuffy.

"How come?" Shenka squeezed me a little closer and her big blue eyes looked down at me. "You've been a good boy, haven't you?"

"Yeah." I didn't want to talk about it. Dad dressed up in a red suit with a white beard to go to his Christmas party. Mom wore green tights and red boots like an elf, too. They wouldn't be back until late, not until I was in bed.

"So you're going to have lots of presents for Christmas tomorrow, aren't you?"

I looked at the pictures in the book again. Big boxes under a tree, people in funny caps they used to wear to bed, and stars and snow outside. I heard Mom say it was supposed to snow tonight, so they wouldn't stay late.

"Can we read more of the story?" My voice felt like nails in my throat.

"Are you all right, Daniel?" Shenka's hand felt cold on my forehead. "Do you have a fever?"

"Uh-uh."

We read until the guy saw the moon on the best of the new-fallen snow. I never get that part. How can part of the snow be better than the other part? Mom told me it was "breast," not best, but that doesn't make any sense, either. Snow isn't a lady like Mom. Or like Shenka. She's a lady, too, almost.

But she plays softball really good. She's shortstop on the high school team. Dad knows her dad from work and that's how she started coming to sit for me last winter. Dad and Mom took me to some of her games last spring. She doesn't look that big, but boy, she hit the ball so far I could hardly see it. She showed me how to bat and catch better last summer, too.

I wrote Santa Claus and asked him for a new bat and glove like Derek Jeter's before Dad told me he's just made up. I was really sad then, but when he brought Shenka back tonight, she brought a long thin package wrapped in green paper with gold designs on it, and a big green bow that has gold running through it, too. The tag had my name on it. I'll bet it's a bat.

I ran upstairs to get my present for her. It's a little heart on a chain and Dad helped me pick it out. He helped me pay for it, too. I wanted to get her something really nice 'cause she's so nice. Dad said I was posolutely absatively right. That's how he talks when he's being funny. Shenka's so pretty I wondered why she was sitting with me on Christmas Eve and not out on a date with some guy.

When she read the part about dry leaves and hurricanes, it felt like I had dry leaves in my throat and I coughed. I couldn't stop for a minute.

"Are you all right, Daniel?"

It hurt too much to say anything. She laid the book on the coffee table and put her hand on my forehead again. The room felt hot, but I was shivering. She pulled the comforter from the back of the couch and wrapped it around me.

"Let me make something to help you feel better."

"I don't want anything." My voice felt thin as a wire. "I don't like medicine."

When I have to take medicine, Mom hides it in candy or ice cream, even my Flintstones vitamins. But I still know it's there. Yuck.

"This isn't medicine," she said. "Let me go get it started, then we will finish the story, all right?"

She wrapped the comforter around me nice and tight and glided through the dining room arch in her tight blue jeans and fuzzy white sweater so she looked pretty as Mom. Dad says she looks really hot, but I was the one who felt hot and cold at the same time. Through the window, I saw white floating around the streetlight at the end of our driveway. After a minute, I knew it was starting to snow, little tiny flakes. I could hardly see them except around the light.

I didn't even hear Shenka come back until she helped me sit up again and I felt really heavy. She stuck the thermometer under my tongue. When she pulled it out, her eyes turned sad.

"Oh, Daniel, I think you are coming down with a cold. And on Christmas Eve."

She hugged me and I was afraid I'd give it to her, too. I could feel the soft bumps under her sweater while she read about Santa Claus getting to work and filling all the stockings. I wanted to ask her to skip that part because it made my eyes feel all gooey, but I figured it would mess up the rest of the story, so I just watched the fire getting smaller in the fireplace and listened to her voice snipping in my ear. I know the story pretty well, anyway, and it felt good laying against her.

"Happy Christmas to all and to all a good night." She held the book open in her lap and I looked at the picture of Santa Claus and his reindeer flying toward the big white moon and felt bad again because he wasn't real. When I looked out the window, the street-light looked like a big white moon, too, with snow falling around it. The ground was already white.

Shenka went to the kitchen and came back with a cup and saucer. I could see steam coming from the cup.

"Shenka, I'm too little to drink coffee."

She helped me sit up again.

"It is not coffee, Daniel." Her voice sounded soft like Mom's. "It will make your throat feel better. Just take a few sips."

"I don't like medicine."

"Silly." She gave me a big smile and she looked even prettier than Mom, even prettier than Santa's elf. But there's no Santa, so I guess she looked prettier than anything I could think of. My head felt like I had rocks in it.

"It is not medicine," she said. "It is warm tea, and I put in it some honey. It will make your sore throat feel better."

"I don't like tea." I didn't know that, but I don't like to try new things. It's like when she made me change how I held the bat last summer to help me hit better. It felt strange at first, but it worked, so maybe this would work, too.

"Just try a little, Daniel, okay? For me?"

She held it close and I felt the steam go up my nose and it felt sort of good. I tried to breathe through my nose, but it was hard and I couldn't smell anything any more, not even Shenka's fresh smell.

I blew on it a few times until the steam went away. I couldn't taste much but it felt good sliding down my throat. Shenka gave me a big smile.

"Good boy." That made me think of the stocking that wasn't hung by the chimney with care and I felt myself sniffle again. "Try a little more, okay?"

I did. She put another log in the fireplace and a few minutes later a little flame started peeking over it. It made me sleepy to watch it. I can stay up until eight-thirty when there's no school, but I already felt tired and it was only seven-twenty-five. It was snowing even harder, and I wondered when Mom and Dad would come home.

"Daniel, why don't we get you some cookies and get you ready for bed."

I almost asked if I could pour a glass of milk for Santa Claus and put some cookies out for him, too, but then I remembered.

"Okay."

Mom made her special chocolate chip Christmas cookies, but I couldn't even taste them. I only had one and it hurt to swallow. Shenka watched me push the plate away and hugged me again.

"Daniel, I don't think your parents will mind if you don't have a bath tonight because you are ill. Let us get you into a nice warm bed so you can rest and feel better for Christmas."

She watched me brush my teeth and left me in the bathroom alone to get into my pajamas. When I came out, she'd put another blanket on my bed and she tucked it in around me. I still felt myself shivering. I looked out my window at the garage and the empty swimming pool with the cover over it, snowflakes getting bigger and floating around in the light between the garage doors. Shenka pulled the shade down most of the way so the light was just a little box on the far wall. She leaned down and brushed her lips across my forehead and left me nestled all snug in my bed.

"Try to sleep, Daniel. If you need anything, I will be right downstairs until your parents get home."

It was bad enough waiting for Christmas, but even worse knowing that Santa Claus wasn't going to come. My clock ticked as loud as a hammer and kept me awake. I tried reading some of my comic books, even though I'd read them all before, but my eyes were all yucked up so the pictures looked blurry and I finally dropped them next to my slippers. I put my head down but it was hard to breathe so I watched the square of light on my wall like it was a movie. I tried to remember *How The Grinch Stole Christmas* and watch that, but my eyes didn't work and my breathing filled up the whole room.

I wondered if Shenka was watching a DVD downstairs or reading a book. Maybe she was eating a cookie for me. At least I knew she got me the bat I wanted, and that made me feel a little better.

When my clock said it was almost midnight and Santa Claus should have been landing on the roof, Dad's headlights flashed on the garage and I heard him stop near the back door. He and Mom stamped the snow off their boots on the back porch before they came in.

A few minutes later, the car pulled out again and I knew Dad was driving Shenka home. She must have told them I was sick because Mom came into my room a minute later. She was still wearing her elf costume, her red sweater with candy canes and the green tights. Her dark curls had a few white snowflakes melting in them.

"Honey, are you all right? Shenka said you weren't feeling well."

"I'm okay." My throat burned and the words came out so soft I don't think she even heard me.

She had a bottle of Robitussin and a spoon. Yuck. She felt my forehead.

"Shenka said she took your temperature and you had a little fever. She gave you some tea and honey. Did it help any?"

"A little," I whispered. I didn't care if it was Christmas eve or not. There was no Santa Claus and I felt sick. I just wanted to close my eyes and wake up all better. Then I remembered I wouldn't be able to try out the bat Shenka gave me until spring anyway. I wondered if Mom and Dad got me a new glove, too. Maybe Shenka told them I wanted one like Derek Jeter's.

"Let's give you some of this," Mom said.

She waited with the spoon until I opened my mouth and she could slide it in. I couldn't even taste it.

I guess I finally fell asleep, but then I started coughing and couldn't stop and it woke me up again. Mom came in wearing her nightgown and robe. She got me a glass of water and watched me drink the whole thing down. Then she hugged me.

I rolled over and looked past the glowing numbers on my clock and out the window. The snow was drifting over the swimming pool cover and making the light on the garage look like a big puffy cloud.

Mom looked out the window, too.

"What do you hope Santa brings you most tomorrow, Daniel?"

My eyes blurred up again. "Dad says there's no Santa Claus."

Mom made a face. She was still looking out the window. "Forget what Dad says. What do you want most of all?"

"A bat," I said. I figured it was safe to wish for that because I knew Shenka got me one.

Just then, I heard a car coming down the driveway and the lights reflected off the garage door so the box of light moved across my wall.

My clock said it was after two o'clock and Mom said something about some kind of pitch. I didn't think she liked baseball that much. I heard her feet on the stairs, real heavy. A minute later, I heard the back door open.

The light over the garage was like the moon on the best of the falling snow, and I saw Mom walk toward the garage with something shiny in one hand and the long green package behind her back. I could see her nightgown below her coat, almost down to her boots. Dad eased out of his car and she met him after he closed the garage door. Even though there was no such thing as Santa Claus, he was still wearing his costume.

Mom handed him the shiny thing and he tipped it up to his mouth. It was the flask he drank liquor from.

He took a long drink and when he took his hand away from his mouth, Mom swung that green package at him. She stepped forward with her left foot, the way Shenka taught me to do, and led with her hips and kept both hands together. She let her arms stretch out as long as they could, and her shoulders turned with her hands so the package was a green blur in the snow-filled light.

The snow was so thick it was like watching through fog, but I saw Dad's head snap back. He dropped his flask and stumbled back a step, then he fell through the swimming pool cover and into the deep end, near the diving board.

Mom stood there looking at the empty spot for a minute, then she held Shenka's package up and looked at it from one end to the other. Snow was coming down so hard I could hardly see her as she looked at the garage, down at the flask, and at the swimming pool. Then she walked back toward the house and I pulled the covers around me before she saw me looking out my window.

When I went downstairs the next morning, it was still snowing and there was a fire in the fireplace. Mom was in jeans and her red and green Christmas sweater, the one with snowmen all over it.

"Merry Christmas, honey." She gave me a big hug. "How do you feel?"

My throat was still sore and my eyes were sticky. I sat on the couch and looked in the fireplace, where a bundle of green paper burned along with a log. At one end of the mantel, I saw my stocking on the nail above the fireplace, and it was bulging full, round and thick like a catcher's mitt.

"Where's Dad?"

Mom put my stocking on the table in front of me. "He must have stayed at Shenka's parents' house because of the snow."

When I looked out the window, I couldn't even see Dad's tire tracks from last night. Or where Mom went out to meet him. Maybe she didn't go out there after all. Maybe I just dreamed it because I was sick.

Mom put my other presents on the coffee table so I could sit on the couch and open them.

She reached under the tree and picked up a long thin package. The tag had Shenka's writing, but now the paper was shiny red with pictures of Santa Claus all over it.

"I'll bet you know what this is, so why don't you open it first."

Sure enough, it was a bat, just the kind I wanted. I stood up and held it high, the way Shenka showed me. It felt good in my hands, like something alive and strong. I wanted to try it out, but I couldn't, not in the house.

"How nice," Mom said. "You should call her later and thank her."

"I will."

I wondered if Shenka had opened the gold heart on a chain that Dad and I got for her. I'd ask when I called to thank her for my bat.

Mom watched me opening the presents from my stocking. She pulled a tissue from the box on the table for me and wiped her eyes.

"I hope I'm not getting your cold."

I got a baseball glove, too, a Derek Jeter one, just like Shenka's. Even with my cold, I could smell it, like a whole room full of shoes.

When I'd opened all my presents, Dad still wasn't there.

Mom dialed her cell phone. When Shenka's dad came on, she wished him Merry Christmas.

"Is Ted over there still? Oh. I see. No, but it was snowing pretty hard when he left here with your daughter last night, so I wondered…"

There's no such person as Santa Claus, so he couldn't be lying in the deep end of our swimming pool. Besides, who ever heard of Santa Claus swimming?

Mom listened to the voice on the other end for a minute, her eyes drifting beyond our Christmas tree and out the window toward the garage.

"Could you put Shenka on for a minute?" Her eyes looked back at me. "Daniel wants to thank her for the baseball bat."

Steve Liskow (www.steveliskow.com) is a former actor, theatrical director, and English teacher whose short stories have earned an Edgar nomination and the Black Orchid Novella Award. Many of his novels take place in his home state of Connecticut and feature issues including teen trafficking and a shooting at a public school. *Blood on the Tracks* (2013) introduces Detroit PI Chris "Woody" Guthrie and draws on Steve's experience as a guitarist and DJ. The book won Honorable Mention for the Writer's Digest Self-Published Novel Awards in 2014.

THE CASE OF THE ADDLETON TRAGEDY

by Jack Grochot

Sherlock Holmes was ecstatic when he returned to our rooms at Baker Street after a morning of investigating the bizarre death of Sir Reginald Abercrombe, who was recklessly riding a galloping horse through a neighborhood in Kilburn and fell lifeless from the saddle in the back yard of Mrs Mortimer Snead. The animal kept running and made its way back to the livery stable, leaving the outstretched corpse of Sir Reginald on the lawn for a terrified Mrs Snead to discover when she went out to dry her linens on the laundry line.

One of Scotland Yard's most inexperienced inspectors, Joseph Kennedy, called on Holmes just after breakfast to ask for his assistance in unraveling the mystery of how Sir Reginald met his abrupt end.

"It was a simple matter of deduction, Watson, a mere distraction from my regular work," the consulting detective confidently informed me. "The hoof prints in the grass directly under the clothes line were a clear indication that Sir Reginald hung himself without a thought of the danger in his behavior. A trip to the livery stable confirmed that he had rented a horse for the day and that it arrived home minus its rider. An examination of the cadaver at the hospital revealed that Sir Reginald died of a crushed windpipe. Case closed. Now here is the most interesting tidbit: The horse he rode was none other than Silver Blaze, racing champion of the Wessex Cup in Dartmoor, whose disappearance I solved and which you so fluently chronicled with your penchant toward exaggeration. I recognized Silver Blaze instantly when I visited the stable and found him in cross-ties while being groomed by the manager. As the hostler explained it, Silver Blaze suffered a bowed tendon in a subsequent contest and was retired. The owner learned that Silver Blaze, unfortunately, was unable to breed, so he sold him for a pittance to his friend, the livery stable manager, who nursed Silver

Blaze back to soundness, but by then he was too old and too fragile to compete again."

"All of which proves that fame is a fleeting condition," I responded philosophically in reaction to the news. "As for the problem of Sir Reginald, I can only say it is fortuitous that it was resolved in a few hours, knowing that you are juggling several investigations at once in this, your busiest year, since I sold my practice in Kensington and moved back to our shared diggings."

Having made that observation, I was reluctant to burden Holmes with a conundrum of my own—yet it bothered me so greatly that I spoke up, despite my misgivings, to solicit his advice.

"Yesterday afternoon," I began hesitantly as he sat comfortably in the wicker basket-chair, "the postman delivered a distressing letter to me concerning a predicament of my former commanding officer in the second Afghan war, Captain Ichabod Addleton."

"What sort of predicament—anything that might require my services?" Holmes asked graciously, pretending not to be preoccupied.

"It seems that Captain Addleton has been driven out of his good senses by a calamity, the simultaneous deaths of his wife and daughter," I answered gravely. I rose from the desk and handed Holmes the correspondence, explaining that it was from the captain's sister, with whom he was living in Blackwall. "I never met her, but the captain apparently mentioned me to her before he dropped into the abyss," I went on.

"Her penmanship is exquisite," Holmes commented as he glanced at the two pages of stationery. "She must be considerably younger than he." Holmes read aloud:

"'Dear Dr Watson,

"'I am writing to you out of desperation and concern for my brother, Ichabod Addleton, who once told me of your remarkable published article in a medical journal regarding the complexities of the human brain. I am afraid my brother has lost his mind, and perhaps you can help restore his sanity.

"'Ichabod sank into deep depression after a fire at his home in Knight's Place killed his loving wife, Annabelle, and his only child, Daphne, who was only twenty-two years old and betrothed to a soldier in Her Majesty's Palace Guard. The victims were overcome by smoke and perished in their beds, while Ichabod escaped the flames because he was away that night at the Veterans' Club playing cards.

"'His depression led to delusions, and now he confines himself to his rooms on my second floor, thinking that he is William Shakespeare and composing the same lines of a play over and over.

"'I have consulted a therapist, who conducted an interview with my brother, and he came to the conclusion that Ichabod believed himself responsible for the demise of his family. The therapist, Dr Michael Paquet, stated to me that the situation seemed hopeless, because he could not convince my brother that the disaster was accidental due to a faulty chimney attached to the fireplace, just as the police had theorised.

"'I implore you, Dr Watson, to come talk to Ichabod and see if you can make progress where Dr Paquet could not. My brother might respond to you in a more positive way, because he respects and admires your heroic efforts in Afghanistan, as well as the reputation you have earned since your honourable discharge from the military.

"'Yours truly,

"'Amanda Addleton'"

Sherlock Holmes shrugged his bony shoulders as he stood to hand back the letter, but otherwise showed no emotion. "It is brief and to the point, Watson, although it leaves questions unanswered, such as why your Captain Addleton would consider himself to blame. We should go there in the morning to find out for ourselves," Holmes offered.

"But what of your other cases—would not a journey to Blackwall interfere with your schedule?" I countered.

"If it means helping a dear friend settle a difficulty, my schedule can accommodate a day's delay," he said sincerely. "Now tell me what you know of the captain and the therapist, Dr Paquet."

I explained that Captain Addleton was in charge of my regimental unit in the Fifth Northumberland Fusiliers from the time I joined the medical corps as an assistant surgeon until a short time after I was seriously wounded in 1880. I remembered how Captain Addleton sat sympathetically at my bedside many times in the field hospital, barking out strict orders to the nurses about my care and encouraging me to lightly exercise to improve the circulation in my limbs. I also recalled the conversations we had regarding our kin back in England. I related to Holmes that it was during those chats that the captain told me stories about his young daughter and about the hardship of separation from his Annabelle. He would describe his magnificent stone house near Twickenham Green and the immense fireplace that warmed the entire downstairs, except for the kitchen, where Annabelle kept a woodstove burning and cooked or baked all day to her heart's content. He fondly referred to their housekeeper, a quick-tempered girl in her late teens, who treated Annabelle like the mother she always wanted but was denied because the woman died in childbirth. The youthful servant, he said compassionately, lived with her quarrelsome father in a nearby apartment, but she detested the arrangement because he never forgave her for the fate of his wife.

Additionally, I informed Holmes that Captain Addleton and I maintained contact by post after we left the service, but the occasional communications dwindled to nothing over the last few years.

"As for Dr Paquet," I continued, "the physician's directory cites his work with patients diagnosed as schizophrenic and delusionary. He studied under the noted Swiss psychiatrist Paul Eugen Bleuler, the author of numerous monographs on the subject of mental illness."

"What you tell me about the captain is suggestive," Holmes observed, without elaborating. "And Dr Paquet seems competent enough, but he gives up too easily. You can accomplish more than he, I am certain."

We were interrupted in our discussion by a familiar footstep on the stairs. Our landlady, Mrs Hudson, entered our rooms to bring us a hot pot of tea and freshly-made crumpets, with a word of rapprochement for Holmes. "You haven't been eating properly because of all your comings and goings lately, so here is a snack to tide you over until dinner," she said thoughtfully. "And don't you run off this evening, for I am making a special supper, chicken pot pies and mashed potatoes, one of your favourites. That will put some meat back on your skinny frame."

We thanked her profusely and she accepted our gratitude with a slight smile, a nod, and a grunt; then she exited the flat after quickly inspecting the curtains in our sitting-room. "I need to wash these soon—your pipe and cigar smoke has turned them yellow," she remarked.

After we ate the mid-day treat, Holmes went off on one of his capers, in disguise as an elderly mendicant with a salt-and-pepper beard and a pair of spectacles that had a crack diagonally across one of the lenses. I used the time while he was gone to complete my notes on a recent investigation Holmes had finished success-fully involving the theft of the Bishopgate jewel collection.

Holmes returned to our quarters just in time to partake of Mrs Hudson's delicious meal, he still in costume. It startled our land-lady when she saw him seated at the table and for a moment she thought a street beggar was there in his place.

Later, after I had scoured the pages of the evening *Star* that our news agent delivered, I went up to bed, leaving Holmes in his lavender dressing gown engrossed in his reference books. I was restless and slept fitfully, dreaming and awakening to images of the bleeding troops in the Afghanistan campaign.

Morning came with a violent thunderstorm, so after we had toast and coffee, we donned our slickers and caught a London growler to Charing Cross Station for a train to the eastern terminus of the railway in Blackwall. By the time we reached our destina-tion, knowing the address from the letter sent by Miss Addleton, the weather had improved, so we draped our slickers over our arms and approached the front door of the two-storey brick dwelling. Neatly-trimmed hedges, dripping with rain, surrounded the house and lined the walkway.

Amanda Addleton greeted me like a long-lost relative after I introduced myself, and she was amazed to meet Holmes, about whom she had learned from the magazine articles I had penned. I guessed Miss Addleton to be in her early forties. She wore her san-dy-coloured hair braided in pig-tails, which accented her tiny ears and round face to the point that it made her appear unattractive. Her flowered dress was loose-fitting, save for the section around her wide hips.

"How is your brother?" I asked after we exchanged pleasantries.

"Physically, he seems fine, although he has lost weight since he relocated here. But his mental state is deteriorating," she an-swered. "When I call him Ichabod or Captain, he sloughs me off and says Captain Ichabod Addleton is in his grave, strung up on the gallows for murdering his wife and daughter. 'My name is William, William Shakespeare,' he retorts. Then he goes back to his sheets of foolscap, repeatedly writing 'O, ye scoundrel! Hath ye no shame?' Occasionally, he cries—sobs, actually—and I can hear him all the way down here. He is a tortured soul now, once a brilliant tactician."

She pleaded with me to try harder than Dr Paquet to revive her brother, suggesting that when we went face-to-face his memory of our association might shock him back to reality. I started up the steps to his rooms and listened at the door to the sound of a man moaning. I rapped gently and heard him tell me to come in.

"Who are *you*?" he demanded, and rose from the desk chair.

"I am your former charge in the Army unit, Dr John H Watson," I replied, surprised at how unkind the years had been to him.

"And so you are. So you are, John. Put on a few pounds and turned grey around the temples, eh?" he noted. "I've been dead for almost two years now, executed for killing my darling Annabelle and my beautiful Daphne. I have been re-incarnated as William Shakespeare and I am writing a drama that depicts the life of Captain Addleton. I am stuck, though, at the beginning. I can't seem to get past the opening lines. See for yourself." He extended his hand, which held a sheet of foolscap, and paused for me to grasp it and read. "You are a writer, John, tell me what you recommend."

"But I don't understand," I said. "Who is the scoundrel?"

"Why, it is Captain Addleton, of course," he shot back.

"What makes him a scoundrel?"

The captain stiffened. "I can't tell you that—it is a secret," he responded curtly.

"Well, then, if you won't reveal the secret, I don't see how I can help you get beyond the opening lines," I blurted.

He sat down at the desk again. "It is time for you to leave, John. I have things to do," he concluded, and buried his head in the papers that were scattered in front of him.

I went downstairs to relay the details of the short repartee to Holmes and Miss Addleton, who were in the dining room having tea. I shared a cup with them and was charmed when Miss Addleton praised my results as a minor breakthrough. Holmes gathered from my description of the dialogue that the guilt the captain harboured stemmed from an incident or a chapter in his marriage, which he wanted no one to discover.

"What propelled him over the edge, Watson, was the content of a parcel Miss Addleton recalls him receiving soon after he arrived here," Holmes disclosed, adding that the package was left on the front stoop during the night and contained only the name Ichabod on the wrapping. "It felt heavy, as if it were a large book," Miss Addleton further remembered.

"I saw a volume on his desk entitled *A History of the Royal Army,*" I interjected.

"Oh, my word!" exclaimed Miss Addleton. "That was a cherished birthday gift to him from Annabelle! But how did he acquire it? He came to live with me with only the clothes on his back. He had no belongings—they were all lost in the fire."

"The book must have been what you found on your doorstep," Sherlock Holmes stated to her. "It probably was salvaged from the ruins of the home at Knight's Place, but by whom? Watson, please go upstairs and ask Captain Addleton if you can borrow the history briefly. Perhaps it has some inscription that would shed light on this little puzzle."

I did as he asked, and when I requested the loan of the book, Captain Addleton informed me that it was too precious to remove from his sight, because his wife had sent it to him from the Great Beyond. To prove it, he showed me this scribbled message on the flyleaf:

"Ichabod,

"Here is your treasured history book that was spared by the fire. Come join me, for I shall love you through eternity." There was no signature below the words.

I hurried downstairs and reported my findings.

"Obviously, the captain has a female admirer, but he is confused and can't fathom the book came from her, not his deceased wife," Holmes commented. "Imagine the irony if the book and the inscription pushed him over the brink."

Miss Addleton was aghast at the concept of her brother being romantically linked to another woman. "He was devoted to Annabelle. It is possible, is it not, that he rejected the love of this other woman?" Miss Addleton queried rhetorically.

"Anything is possible," Holmes replied soothingly. "But I suspect we have unearthed Captain Addleton's secret."

"Well, what do we do now?" she said, whimpering.

"To confront him today with the prospect of knowing about his private horror would likely do more harm than good," I chimed in. "We have penetrated into his dark world deep enough for now. My friend and I will be leaving, but I can return in a few days to see the captain again. Besides, I need some time to think about the next session with him."

Holmes agreed, and so we departed after I patted her softly on the forearm.

Once we were outside, Holmes suggested we take the train to Windsor Station and walk to Knight's Place so he could satisfy his curiosity about the fire at the captain's former residence.

"What do you expect to find there?" I wanted to know.

"Perhaps something the official police overlooked, or maybe a clue to the identity of the other woman—a piece of information that would aid you in your future conversations with Captain Addleton," he speculated.

Our walk from Windsor Station, which was crowded with tourists, took us through mews and streets with park-like qualities until we reached Knight's Place, where the great stone house of the Addleton family stood abandoned with its roof collapsed and window frames charred from the thick smoke.

Holmes led the way in by shoving open the burned front door, which was ajar. "Be careful here, Watson, for the floor might not be intact," he warned. Once inside, we marveled at the destruction of a once-comfortable drawing room, with paneled walls that were scorched so badly that we could not determine what kind of wood had covered the blocks of stone. We cautiously made our way past a huge fireplace with a granite mantel and into a dining hall, the ceiling of which was caved in, causing the chandelier to crash and shatter atop a table so large that a host could entertain a dozen dinner guests. Miraculously, the remainder of the floor was left untouched by the blaze, including the relatively small library, where Captain Addleton's female admirer must have salvaged the history book.

Upstairs, every part of the hallway connecting the bedrooms was covered in soot, even the interiors of the rooms and their furniture, which were otherwise unscathed. "Curiously, Watson, the fire seems to have been concentrated in the two lower rooms—not up here where a faulty chimney would have done the most damage," Holmes observed. "Let's make a closer inspection of the drawing room."

As we descended to the bottom of the staircase, Holmes got down on his hands and knees to examine the baseboard with his magnifying glass. "Hmmm. Ah ha," he said under his breath. He followed the glass all along the baseboard to the fireplace, repeating, "Ah ha," then stood erect. "My suspicions were correct, Watson," he announced finally in a low voice. "This fire was the handiwork of an arsonist. The burn pattern on the baseboard is in the form of splashes—see here, and there, and over here. An accelerant, probably lamp oil, was used to ignite the flames. As usual, the authorities botched the job, and because of their bungling, a double-homicide has gone unpunished."

"The captain!" I shouted excitedly. "He insists that he murdered his wife and daughter!"

"That has yet to be determined, but it does undoubtedly cast Ichabod Addleton in an inauspicious light," Holmes postulated. "Come, we shall have a further look in the library, but be wary of where you step—the floor is weak in spots."

I asked Holmes as we gingerly approached the study if we should go to Scotland Yard with the information. "If justice is to be served, I believe that is our only alternative," he said reluctantly. Once inside the library, Holmes was drawn immediately to the hand-carved, grimy, mahogany desk, and he began opening the drawers after first examining the miscellaneous papers on top. "Nothing of interest to us here so far," he judged. He came upon a locked bottom drawer and opened it easily with the barrel-and- bit key he always carried on a ring attached to his trouser belt loop.

Inside the drawer was the captain's service revolver, resting on several pieces of correspondence. Holmes dropped his hand in, placed the revolver on the desktop, removed the letters, and started at once poring over them. "The first one is from Annabelle," he revealed, "telling her husband, affectionately, how much she and Daphne appreciated the opportunity he gave them to visit their relatives on the Continent over an extended period. These other four are steamy love notes with a distinctly different style of handwriting than Annabelle's. Compare them, Watson, to the handwriting you saw on the flyleaf of the history book."

"It appears to match," I told Holmes, regretfully, after I glanced over his shoulder.

He placed the weapon back in the drawer, neatly folded the correspondence, and tucked it into his inside jacket pocket. "Enough of this burglary business," he intoned, "for we have a solemn duty to convey the facts to the Yard."

We rode in a hansom to the headquarters of the Metropolitan Police Service at Whitehall Place and went through the rear public entrance, where Holmes requested a meeting with Inspector Tobias Gregson. Holmes had once described him as the smartest of the Scotland Yarders, quick, energetic, but conventional. "With Inspector Gregson," Holmes said to me while we waited, "we have as good a chance as any for a reasonable discussion. It is a delicate task for an outsider to instruct the authorities on how they went wrong."

After a short while, Inspector Gregson appeared in the lobby and clasped Holmes's hand warmly, saying it had been a long time since their last encounter. "Dr Watson, I have been reading your accounts of your confederate's triumphs, but I'm eager to learn about one of his failures, too," he said to me, smiling.

"They are few and far between, and not nearly as intriguing," I retorted.

We accompanied him to his office, and once inside, he addressed Holmes. "I assume this is not a social call, so what can I do for you?"

Diplomatically, Holmes explained the situation in detail, after which Tobias Gregson excused himself to look up the file on the fire at Knight's Place. When he returned in more than a few moments, his expression was dour. "I apologise for the delay, gentlemen," he began, "but I had to assure myself that our records were accurate. It seems there was no investigation of the deaths because the constables on the scene made the determination that the fatalities were accidental due to an accumulation of creosote in the lower portion of the chimney. Among us, I consider this negligent. However, it can be rectified. I shall report our conversation to my superiors and I believe a probe will ensue now. I thank you both for bringing this matter to my attention."

On the way out, Holmes inquired if I carried my discharge card from the Army.

"I have it in my wallet, as always," I answered.

"Excellent," he said. "You can escort me as a guest for dinner at the Veterans' Club. This is a Monday. Miss Addleton advised me that her brother played cards with a regular group of close friends every Monday and Friday night. We shall interrogate those friends tonight and ascertain if her brother can establish an iron-clad alibi for the date on which the tragedy occurred. If he cannot, I fear his destiny is sealed."

The menu at the club was limited but appetising. Holmes and I ordered the beef brisket with buttered potatoes and broccoli, then shared a decanter of brandy afterward to await the gathering of comrades at the gaming tables in the recreation room off the dining hall. Our waiter pointed out the cluster of men with whom Captain Addleton once had enjoyed rounds of poker until the club closed at midnight. Holmes approached them and politely begged their pardon for interrupting, then informed them of his purpose for asking his questions.

Three of the participants remembered that a police sergeant intruded on their game the night of the fire and broke the news to Captain Addleton that his wife and daughter had died from smoke inhalation. "Ichabod was rattled and slumped in his chair," recalled one of the men, a Mr Wetherington. "He had been here the entire time until then, which was about eleven-thirty," Mr Wetherington stated positively. "It was such a shock, I shall never forget it—I knew both women, had been to their home," he lamented. "I understand that Ichabod is still grieving."

"Yes, he stays with his sister in Blackwall and never leaves his rooms," Holmes confirmed.

"Pity. We could do with his wit again," Mr Wetherington confessed, remorseful that his companion had been absent so long.

"Tell me, if you would," Holmes went on, "did Mr Addleton ever mention that he had an enemy, or was there someone who held a grudge against him?"

They all shook their heads no.

"Did he ever talk of any women in his life besides his wife and daughter?" Holmes wanted to know.

"Now see here!" a Mr Price protested. "Just what do you mean to imply by that question?"

Before Holmes could respond, Mr Wetherington named Sally, the Addletons's housekeeper. "Ichabod would sometimes regale us with her shenanigans," he related, then grinned. "She was like a second daughter to him. I met her also when I visited Ichabod—a raving beauty, she is."

After a few parting words, Holmes and I boarded the Underground for our trip back to Baker Street, where he decided during a chat in the sitting-room that identifying the arsonist was more urgent than any of his other pending cases. "They are incidental when contrasted against this one," he allowed.

And so it was early the next morning that we took the train again to Blackwall, where Miss Addleton apprised us of the whereabouts of Sally, whose last name was Wiggins. After the fire, Sally went to work as a fashion model for Herrod's Department Store in Stafford, having vacated the apartment she shared with her grumpy father and moved in with a roommate at a flat on Priory Street in the East End. Holmes and I next traveled to Stafford to interview the young woman, and we were ushered by the store proprietor to his finely decorated suite on the fifth floor.

"At the moment," he said, "Miss Wiggins is showing a new line of gowns from Paris to a group of ladies belonging to the Westminster Society. I can arrange for her to come here afterward. In the meantime, gentlemen, please help yourselves to some coffee or tea over there on the salver."

Soon, she appeared in the doorway, and we both rose, cups in hand and stunned by her elegance—long, wavy blond hair caressing her shoulders, sparkling blue eyes, an angelic face with an upturned nose, and a perfectly curved figure that fitted tightly into a flattering, pale-green evening dress, which sensuously flowed over her bare ankles.

Holmes, charming her with a compliment, spoke of the purpose of our calling, and she reacted with distress. "The murder of Annabelle and Daphne?" she repeated breathlessly. "I can't understand. Who would want to kill Annabelle and Daphne?"

"And possibly the man of the house, as well," Holmes added. "Not many people knew he would be away playing cards the night the fire was set."

"Oh, good Lord," Miss Wiggins ejaculated. "They hadn't a foe in the world. Who would do such a thing?"

"That is what I hope you can assist us in discovering," Holmes told her.

"Assist you how?" she inquired.

"By sitting down at a table when you go home today and writing a list of all the people the family knew or who had been to their house," Holmes stated. "Here is my address," he said, tearing a sheet from his notebook. "You can send the list to me there as quickly as you are able."

"I shall make your request a priority, Mr Holmes," she promised before gracefully seating herself on the sofa, nervously clutching the slip of paper Holmes had given her.

We left Miss Wiggins composing herself in the proprietor's suite and took the train to Charing Cross, walking the distance from the station to Baker Street while silently mulling over the developments thus far. Earlier, as we rode on the Pullman coach, Holmes offered a perplexing comment that caused me to wonder what he had in mind. "I have two reasons for asking Sally Wiggins to provide me with the data," he admitted. "The first is obvious, and the second is perhaps the solution to this whole affair."

We were eating a late lunch of some leftovers that were in the ice chest when our landlady knocked and entered our rooms after I answered, "Please come in, Mrs Hudson." We knew it was she from the cadence of her rapping. "Peterson, the commissionaire," she announced, "is waiting downstairs for a reply to this message directed to you both." She handed me the note, which came from Miss Addleton.

"Mr Holmes and Dr Watson (it read):

"I have terrible news about my brother. They have carted him off in irons and accused him of murder, telling me that he wanted his wife out of the way so he could be with the other woman.

"Please help him and tell me what I am to do."

"Fools!" Holmes bellowed. "Why would he start a fire that also endangered a daughter he idolized?"

Holmes hastily wrote instructions for Miss Addleton on the reverse side of the message and handed it back to Mrs Hudson. "Here is a half-sovereign for Peterson if he can deliver the reply this afternoon," said Holmes, and, turning to me, asked if I was prepared to have another try at bringing Captain Addleton back to his good senses.

"I've thought about my approach and I think I'm ready," I responded.

"Capital, Watson," he went on, "then let's be off to Scotland Yard, where you can visit the captain in the dock and I can engage Inspector Gregson in a Dutch-uncle talk. I must concede I anticipated this outcome from the conference with him yesterday, but I had hoped he would be more circumspect, rather than rush to judgment."

We arrived at police headquarters just as Tobias Gregson was enlightening the press gathered in the lobby how he had recently uncovered clues that led to solving the cold case.

Afterward, in the privacy of his office, Holmes inquired of the inspector if he knew that Ichabod Addleton had witnesses who could establish his innocence.

"Let him produce a dozen witnesses," Inspector Gregson contended. "I have a star witness to whom the defendant confessed the crime—your biographer, Dr Watson."

"But he is insane; he hallucinates," I interjected. "Does that not reduce his confession to rubbish?"

"He is lucid enough to know right from wrong," the inspector argued. "That is sufficient to render his admission admissible in court, and you, Doctor, are compelled to testify as to what you heard from his own lips."

"What transpires between a patient and his physician is confidential," I debated, realising my argument was a weak one.

"We shall see about that," Inspector Gregson snapped.

Holmes interrupted our dispute with a request that I meet with the captain in the lockup.

The inspector acquiesced. "Of course, by all means," he said gladly. "But be forewarned, I shall want to know what he has to say."

Holmes accompanied me to the cellblock, and we found the prisoner in an agitated state. When I introduced Holmes to Captain Addleton, he was unimpressed until I informed him that Holmes was there to help him attain his freedom.

"That is wonderful," he remarked, "for it is impossible for a playwright to compose his best work in a place like this—no paper, no pen, no table."

"We have learned Captain Addleton's secret!" I proclaimed. "We now know why he was a scoundrel!"

He reacted with a start, then settled. "What is it that you know?" he asked.

"We have discovered that Captain Addleton was unfaithful to his wife; he concealed a lover," I revealed.

"It was not a matter of love. It was a dalliance on his part while his wife was on holiday," William Shakespeare declared. "The other woman took it more seriously, though, and pursued the captain. She became obsessed. She went to extremes. She took drastic measures."

"Who was this other woman? What was her name?" I persisted.

"That is not important, John," he continued. "The harm she inflicted was irreparable. Besides, it was Captain Addleton who was responsible for the catastrophe. It was he who instigated the adultery. O, ye scoundrel! Hath ye no shame?"

Even using other methods, I attempted to accomplish the impossible with the captain, so Holmes and I left him brooding about his confinement. I reported my lack of success to Inspector Gregson and went with Holmes back to our diggings.

Later that afternoon, Billy, a page-boy at Baker Street, brought Holmes an envelope that contained the list Miss Wiggins had drawn up naming associates and acquaintances of the Addleton family.

"As I suspected, Watson," Holmes boasted, "Sally Wiggins is the other woman. Her handwriting is identical to that in those four lurid love notes locked in the bottom desk drawer."

Holmes decided to confront her that very evening at her apartment on Priory Street, but first he wrote a message and asked Mrs Hudson to give it to Billy for delivery immediately. We hailed an empty cab that was passing our building and in five minutes we were taking the stairs down to the Underground terminal. Holmes rode in the train car with his hands clasped behind his head, his dark eyes closed, and his toes tapping in rhythm, as if imagining a tune, but I surmised he was plotting his next strategic move. A half-hour later he was turning the small lever that rang the doorbell at apartment number 4-C.

"Who is it?" came a sweet feminine voice from inside.

"It is Sherlock Holmes and Dr Watson, here to see Miss Wiggins about a pressing matter," Holmes replied.

"She is in the bathtub but won't be much longer," said her roommate. "I'll go tell her who it is. Please wait."

A moment later, the roommate swung open the door. "She said for you to come in and have a seat. She'll be out directly," said the jittery young lady. "It's not often a detective and a doctor come calling. Is something amiss?"

"Don't be upset," Holmes said to reassure her. "Miss Wiggins will explain after we have gone on our way."

"If you say so, I won't worry then," the roommate remarked. "I must excuse myself and leave this instant or I will be late for a dinner engagement with my beau. He adores it that I am punctual." With that, the young lady departed in a flash.

In time, Miss Wiggins emerged from the bath, drying her wet, stringy hair with a towel and appearing far less elegant than she did at work. Now without makeup and wearing a bulky, white terry-cloth robe over plaid pajamas, she flopped down into an armchair and brusquely asked: "Did you bring me news of a revelation in your investigation?"

"In a manner of speaking, yes, I did," answered Holmes coyly.

"My list was helpful, then," she glowed.

"Yes, it was, in a way you didn't expect," he went on.

"What on earth do you mean?" she inquired.

"Perhaps if you would be more forthcoming, I could explain myself in more explicit terms," he added.

"What are you getting at, Mr Holmes," Miss Wiggins demanded.

"What I am getting at is this, my dear," Sherlock Holmes began. "You and Ichabod Addleton were entwined in a love triangle. You were jealous of Annabelle, because Mr Addleton refused to divorce her. You threatened to eliminate the wife if you couldn't marry him, and you carried out that threat by setting the house ablaze on a night you knew Mr Addleton would be away."

"Prove it," she said calmly.

"I intend to, Miss Wiggins. Here are four love notes in your handwriting, graphically depicting your intimacy," said Holmes, spreading the correspondence on the coffee table that stood between them. "In one of these notes, you frankly state: 'If I can't have you, Ichabod, I'll fix it so she can't have you either.' It is dated two days before the fire. I have sent a message requesting Inspector Gregson of Scotland Yard to come here at seven o'clock with a writ to search your flat. I shall hazard a guess that he and his men will locate a skeleton key that fits the rim lock on the door to the servants' entrance at the former Addleton residence. Also, they will find incriminating evidence in a diary on your nightstand, a memoir of your life's events which I perused while you were bathing. After all is said and done, the authorities might still retain Mr Addleton in custody, because they could regard him as a co-conspirator."

"He is in jail?" she whined.

"He has been arrested for the murder of his wife and daughter," Holmes informed her.

"Oh, God, no! They'll hang him!" Miss Wiggins sputtered. She bent forward, buried her troubled countenance in the palms of her hands, and burst into tears, totally losing control of herself. "I still love him with all my heart," she heaved. Then, after a period of quiet, she thrust herself upward in a daze. "But they won't hang a woman, will they?" she wondered, glaring at Holmes. She answered her own question: "No, they won't. It's me the police want, Mr Holmes. Don't let them hang him for what I alone did. He is faultless, an innocent, broken man. Oh, Ichabod, my poor, poor Ichabod." Again, she cried, hysterically.

Some weeks later, Miss Wiggins pleaded guilty to homicide by arson and was sentenced to ten years imprisonment in the women's section at Parkhurst Penitentiary. Captain Addleton never recovered, and, tragically, he died in an asylum at the age of fifty-six.

✗

Jack Grochot is a retired investigative newspaper journalist and a former federal law enforcement agent specializing in mail fraud cases. He lives on a small farm in southwestern Pennsylvania, where he writes and cares for five boarded horses. His fiction work includes the book *Come, Watson! Quickly!*, a collection of five Sherlock Holmes pastiches. He is an active member of Mystery Writers of America.

GOLD-DIGGER

by Laird Long

Sheriff Brown trudged up the hill to Charlie Johnson's shack near the mouth of the old abandoned gold mine at least once a week. He was fond of the elderly prospector, and wanted to make sure she was doing okay.

But on his latest visit, he found Charlie beaten to death behind her shack, the shack itself ransacked. He grimaced and shook his head. He'd always feared something like this would happen to the eccentric old woman, living all by herself out in the wilds.

The sheriff called in his discovery and then made a thorough examination of the area. But he didn't find a single clue as to the identity of the murderer. So when his Deputy arrived, he trotted back down the winding trail to his car and drove the two miles into Grubbin, went straight to the 'mayor's' office.

Sam Hurley was the unofficial mayor of Grubbin. The former mining town was so small it didn't have a real mayor any more. So Hurley appointed himself since he knew the history of the town and surrounding area so well. Sheriff Brown found His Honor in his 'office'—the Star Café on Main Street.

"Charlie's been murdered, Sam," Brown stated, taking a seat at the small table across from Hurley.

"Doggone it all!" Hurley exclaimed. "I told her to move into town many a time, Sheriff! But she was stubborn, still scratching around for gold up in that hill. Who done it? Do you know?"

"Not yet. But I aim to find out. You see any strangers around recently, Sam?"

"Can't miss 'em in a town this size. Especially when I got the best view of the main drag from my mayoralty seat right here in the café." He nodded. "Yesterday. A young fellow drifted in here with a big knapsack on his back. Tall, skinny, scruffy-looking, with long blond hair, blue eyes, and a big ugly scar right across his forehead."

Brown jotted down the description. "What'd he want? Do?"

"Sat down at that table over there," Hurley pointed, "and ordered a cup of coffee and a cheese sandwich. I could see the fellow was lonesome, so I went on over and introduced myself, and we got to talking."

"What about?"

"Well, the town, its history. You know, doing my duty as mayor." Hurley grinned.

"Talk about Charlie?"

Hurley frowned. "Briefly. The fellow asked me if there was still any gold in the area. And I told him—I said, 'No. But old Charlie Johnson is still scratching around for it. Charlie's a prospector, lives in a shack up near the mouth of the old mine.' That's exactly what I said, Sheriff. Not a word more. I hope I didn't—"

"Did he give a name? Say where he was from? Talk to anybody else?"

"No to all three questions, Sheriff. I was the only one in the café at the time, besides Billie the waitress. And after the fellow finished his meal, I saw him walk on out of town."

✗ ✗ ✗ ✗

Sheriff Brown checked with the bus company that ran a coach along the highway through Grubbin. One of the drivers remembered picking up a man matching the description Hurley had provided, then dropping him off at a stop in Digby down the line, on a street full of cheap rooming houses.

Brown found his man at the third house he tried, after the caretaker confirmed the description and showed him to the right room.

"Kyle Stanton?" the sheriff asked, when a tall, skinny, scruffy-looking, blue-eyed blond man with a scar across his forehead answered Brown's knock.

"Yeah?"

"Ever been to Grubbin, Mr. Stanton?"

"No. Why would I—"

"That's lie number one," Brown cut him off. "An old prospector, Charlie Johnson, was murdered just outside of Grubbin. You go up the hill to see Charlie after you talked to the mayor?"

"No! I didn't go up the hill to see her. I didn't kill any Charlie Johnson!"

"That's lie number two. You're under arrest, Stanton."

The man gaped at Sheriff Brown. "What? Why?"

The sheriff succinctly stated his case, "You said you didn't see 'her,' Stanton. The natural assumption on hearing the name 'Charlie Johnson' would be that the old prospector was a man—unless you'd already met her. Let's go."

✗

Laird Long: Big guy, sense of humor; pounds out fiction in all genres. Has appeared in many anthologies and mystery magazines and resides in Winnipeg, Canada.

THE YELLOW FACE

by Sir Arthur Conan Doyle

In publishing these short sketches based upon the numerous cases in which my companion's singular gifts have made us the listeners to, and eventually the actors in, some strange drama, it is only natural that I should dwell rather upon his successes than upon his failures. And this not so much for the sake of his reputation—for, indeed, it was when he was at his wit's end that his energy and his versatility were most admirable—but because where he failed it happened too often that no one else succeeded, and that the tale was left forever without a conclusion. Now and again, however, it chanced that even when he erred the truth was still discovered. I have notes of some half-dozen cases of the kind, the adventure of the Musgrave Ritual and that which I am about to recount are the two which present the strongest features of interest.

Sherlock Holmes was a man who seldom took exercise for exercise's sake. Few men were capable of greater muscular effort, and he was undoubtedly one of the finest boxers of his weight that I have ever seen; but he looked upon aimless bodily exertion as a waste of energy, and he seldom bestirred himself save where there was some professional object to be served. Then he was absolutely untiring and indefatigable. That he should have kept himself in training under such circumstances is remarkable, but his diet was usually of the sparest, and his habits were simple to the verge of austerity. Save for the occasional use of cocaine, he had no vices, and he only turned to the drug as a protest against the monotony of existence when cases were scanty and the papers uninteresting.

One day in early spring he had so far relaxed as to go for a walk with me in the Park, where the first faint shoots of green were breaking out upon the elms, and the sticky spear-heads of the chestnuts were just beginning to burst into their five-fold leaves. For two hours we rambled about together, in silence for the most part, as befits two men who know each other intimately. It was nearly five before we were back in Baker Street once more.

"Beg pardon, sir," said our page-boy as he opened the door. "There's been a gentleman here asking for you, sir."

Holmes glanced reproachfully at me. "So much for afternoon walks!" said he. "Has this gentleman gone, then?"

"Yes, sir."

"Didn't you ask him in?"

"Yes, sir, he came in."

How long did he wait?"

"Half an hour, sir. He was a very restless gentleman, sir, a-walkin' and a-stampin' all the time he was here. I was waitin' outside the door, sir, and I could hear him. At last he outs into the passage, and he cries, 'Is that man never goin' to come?' Those were his very words, sir. 'You'll only need to wait a little longer,' says I. 'Then I'll wait in the open air, for I feel half choked,' says he. 'I'll be back before long.' And with that he ups and he outs, and all I could say wouldn't hold him back."

"Well, well, you did your best," said Holmes as we walked into our room. "It's very annoying, though, Watson. I was badly in need of a case, and this looks, from the man's impatience, as if it were of importance. Hullo! That's not your pipe on the table. He must have left his behind him. A nice old brier with a good long stem of what the tobacconists call amber. I wonder how many real amber mouthpieces there are in London? Some people think that a fly in it is a sign. Well, he must have been disturbed in his mind to leave a pipe behind him which he evidently values highly."

"How do you know that he values it highly?" I asked.

"Well, I should put the original cost of the pipe at seven and sixpence. Now it has, you see, been twice mended, once in the wooden stem and once in the amber. Each of these mends, done, as you observe, with silver bands, must have cost more than the pipe did originally. The man must value the pipe highly when he prefers to patch it up rather than buy a new one with the same money."

"Anything else? I asked, for Holmes was turning the pipe about in his hand and staring at it in his peculiar pensive way. He held it up and tapped on it with his long, thin forefinger, as a professor might who was lecturing on a bone.

"Pipes are occasionally of extraordinary interest," said he. "Nothing has more individuality, save perhaps watches and boot-laces. The indications here, however, are neither very marked nor very important. The owner is obviously a muscular man, left-hand-ed, with an excellent set of teeth, careless in his habits, and with no need to practise economy."

My friend threw out the information in a very offhand way, but I saw that he cocked his eye at me to see if I had followed his reasoning.

"You think a man must be well-to-do if he smokes a seven-shilling pipe?" said I.

"This is Grosvenor mixture at eightpence an ounce," Holmes answered, knocking a little out on his palm. "As he might get an excellent smoke for half the price, he has no need to practise economy."

"And the other points?"

He has been in the habit of lighting his pipe at lamps and gas-jets. You can see that it is quite charred all down one side. Of course a match could not have done that. Why should a man hold a match to the side of his pipe? But you cannot light it at a lamp without getting the bowl charred. And it is all on the right side of the pipe. From that I gather that he is a left-handed man. You hold your own pipe to the lamp and see how naturally you, being right-handed, hold the left side to the flame. You might do it once the other way, but not as a constancy. This has always been held so. Then he has bitten through his amber. It takes a muscular, energetic fellow, and one with a good set of teeth, to do that. But if I am not mistaken I hear him upon the stair, so we shall have something more interest-ing than his pipe to study."

An instant later our door opened, and a tall young man entered the room. He was well but quietly dressed in a dark gray suit and carried a brown wide-awake in his hand. I should have put him at about thirty, though he was really some years older.

"I beg your pardon," said he with some embarrassment, "I sup-pose I should have knocked. Yes, of course I should have knocked. The fact is that I am a little upset, and you must put it all down to that." He passed his hand over his forehead like a man who is half dazed, and then fell rather than sat down upon a chair.

"I can see that you have not slept for a night or two," said Holmes in his easy, genial way. "That tries a man's nerves more than work, and more even than pleasure. May I ask how I can help you?"

"I wanted your advice, sir. I don't know what to do, and my whole life seems to have gone to pieces."

"You wish to employ me as a consulting detective?"

"Not that only. I want your opinion as a judicious man—as a man of the world. I want to know what I ought to do next. I hope to God you'll be able to tell me."

He spoke in little, sharp, jerky outbursts, and it seemed to me that to speak at all was very painful to him, and that his will all through was overriding his inclinations.

"It's a very delicate thing," said he. One does not like to speak of one's domestic affairs to strangers. It seems dreadful to discuss the conduct of one's wife with two men whom I have never seen before. It's horrible to have to do it. But I've got to the end of my tether, and I must have advice."

"My dear Mr Grant Munro—" began Holmes.

Our visitor sprang from his chair. "What!" he cried, "you know my name?"

"If you wish to preserve your incognito," said Holmes, smiling, "I would suggest that you cease to write your name upon the lining of your hat, or else that you turn the crown towards the person whom you are addressing. I was about to say that my friend and I have listened to a good many strange secrets in this room, and that we have had the good fortune to bring peace to many troubled souls. I trust that we may do as much for you. Might I beg you, as time may prove to be of importance, to furnish me with the facts of your case without further delay?"

Our visitor again passed his hand over his forehead, as if he found it bitterly hard. From every gesture and expression I could see that he was a reserved, self-contained man, with a dash of pride in his nature, more likely to hide his wounds than to expose them. Then suddenly, with a fierce gesture of his closed hand, like one who throws reserve to the winds, he began:

"The facts are these, Mr Holmes," said he. "I am a married man and have been so for three years. During that time my wife and I have loved each other as fondly and lived as happily as any two that ever were joined. We have not had a difference, not one, in thought or word or deed. And now, since last Monday, there has suddenly sprung up a barrier between us, and I find that there is something in her life and in her thoughts of which I know as little as if she were the woman who brushes by me in the street. We are estranged, and I want to know why.

"Now there is one thing that I want to impress upon you before I go any further, Mr Holmes. Effie loves me. Don't let there be any mistake about that. She loves me with her whole heart and soul, and never more than now. I know it. I feel it. I don't want to argue about that. A man can tell easily enough when a woman loves him. But there's this secret between us, and we can never be the same until it is cleared."

"Kindly let me have the facts, Mr Munro," said Holmes with some impatience.

"I'll tell you what I know about Effie's history. She was a widow when I met her first, though quite young—only twenty-five. Her name then was Mrs Hebron. She went out to America when she was young and lived in the town of Atlanta, where she married this Hebron, who was a lawyer with a good practice. They had one child, but the yellow fever broke out badly in the place, and both husband and child died of it. I have seen his death certificate. This sickened her of America, and she came back to live with a maiden aunt at Pinner, in Middlesex. I may mention that her husband had left her comfortably off, and that she had a capital of about four thousand five hundred pounds, which had been so well invested by him that it returned an average of seven per cent. She had only been six months at Pinner when I met her; we fell in love with each other, and we married a few weeks afterwards.

"I am a hop merchant myself, and as I have an income of seven or eight hundred, we found ourselves comfortably off and took a nice eighty-pound-a-year villa at Norbury. Our little place was very countrified, considering that it is so close to town. We had an inn and two houses a little above us, and a single cottage at the other side of the field which faces us, and except those there were no houses until you got halfway to the station. My business took me into town at certain seasons, but in summer I had less to do, and then in our country home my wife and I were just as happy as could be wished. I tell you that there never was a shadow between us until this accursed affair began.

"There's one thing I ought to tell you before I go further. When we married, my wife made over all her property to me—rather against my will, for I saw how awkward it would be if my business affairs went wrong. However, she would have it so, and it was done. Well, about six weeks ago she came to me.

"'Jack,' said she, 'when you took my money you said that if ever I wanted any I was to ask you for it.'

"'Certainly,' said I. 'It's all your own.'

"'Well,' said she, 'I want a hundred pounds.'

"I was a bit staggered at this, for I had imagined it was simply a new dress or something of the kind that she was after.

"'What on earth for?' I asked.

"'Oh,' said she in her playful way, 'you said that you were only my banker, and bankers never ask questions, you know.'

"'If you really mean it, of course you shall have the money,' said I.

"'Oh, yes, I really mean it.'

"'And you won't tell me what you want it for?'

"'Some day, perhaps, but not just at present, Jack.'

"So I had to be content with that, though it was the first time that there had ever been any secret between us. I gave her a check, and I never thought any more of the matter. It may have nothing to do with what came afterwards, but I thought it only right to mention it.

"Well, I told you just now that there is a cottage not far from our house. There is just a field between us, but to reach it you have to go along the road and then turn down a lane. Just beyond it is a nice little grove of Scotch firs, and I used to be very fond of strolling down there, for trees are always a neighbourly kind of thing. The cottage had been standing empty this eight months, and it was a pity, for it was a pretty two-storied place, with an old-fashioned porch and a honeysuckle about it. I have stood many a time and thought what a neat little homestead it would make.

"Well, last Monday evening I was taking a stroll down that way when I met an empty van coming up the lane and saw a pile of carpets and things lying about on the grass-plot beside the porch. It was clear that the cottage had at last been let. I walked past it, and then stopping, as an idle man might, I ran my eye over it and wondered what sort of folk they were who had come to live so near us. And as I looked I suddenly became aware that a face was watching me out of one of the upper windows.

"I don't know what there was about that face, Mr Holmes, but it seemed to send a chill right down my back. I was some little way off, so that I could not make out the features, but there was something unnatural and inhuman about the face. That was the impression that I had, and I moved quickly forward to get a nearer view of the person who was watching me. But as I did so the face suddenly disappeared, so suddenly that it seemed to have been plucked away into the darkness of the room. I stood for five minutes thinking the business over and trying to analyze my impressions. I could not tell if the face was that of a man or a woman. It had been too far from me for that. But its colour was what had impressed me most. It was of a livid chalky white, and with something set and rigid about it which was shockingly unnatural. So disturbed was I that I determined to see a little more of the new inmates of the cottage. I approached and knocked at the door, which was instantly opened by a tall, gaunt woman with a harsh, forbidding face.

"'What may you be wantin'?' she asked in a Northern accent.

"'I am your neighbour over yonder,' said I, nodding towards my house. 'I see that you have only just moved in, so I thought that if I could be of any help to you in any—'

"'Aye, we'll just ask ye when we want ye,' said she, and shut the door in my face. Annoyed at the churlish rebuff, I turned my back and walked home. All evening, though I tried to think of other things, my mind would still turn to the apparition at the window and the rudeness of the woman. I determined to say nothing about the former to my wife, for she is a nervous, highly strung woman, and I had no wish that she should share the unpleasant impression which had been produced upon myself. I remarked to her, however, before I fell asleep, that the cottage was now occupied, to which she returned no reply.

"I am usually an extremely sound sleeper. It has been a standing jest in the family that nothing could ever wake me during the night. And yet somehow on that particular night, whether it may have been the slight excitement produced by my little adventure or not I know not, but I slept much more lightly than usual. Half in my dreams I was dimly conscious that something was going on in the room, and gradually became aware that my wife had dressed herself and was slipping on her mantle and her bonnet. My lips were parted to murmur out some sleepy words of surprise or remonstrance at this untimely preparation, when suddenly my half-opened eyes fell upon her face, illuminated by the candle-light, and astonishment held me dumb. She wore an expression such as I had never seen before—such as I should have thought her incapable of assuming. She was deadly pale and breathing fast, glancing furtively towards the bed as she fastened her mantle to see if she had disturbed me. Then thinking that I was still asleep, she slipped noiselessly from the room, and an instant later I heard a sharp creaking which could only come from the hinges of the front door. I sat up in bed and rapped my knuckles against the rail to make certain that I was truly awake. Then I took my watch from under the pillow. It was three in the morning. What on this earth could my wife be doing out on the country road at three in the morning?

"I had sat for about twenty minutes turning the thing over in my mind and trying to find some possible explanation. The more I thought, the more extraordinary and inexplicable did it appear. I was still puzzling over it when I heard the door gently close again, and her footsteps coming up the stairs.

"'Where in the world have you been, Effie?' I asked as she entered.

"She gave a violent start and a kind of gasping cry when I spoke, and that cry and start troubled me more than all the rest, for there was something indescribably guilty about them. My wife had always been a woman of a frank, open nature, and it gave me a chill to see her slinking into her own room and crying out and wincing when her own husband spoke to her.

"'You awake, Jack!' she cried with a nervous laugh. 'Why, I thought that nothing could awake you.'

"'Where have you been?' I asked, more sternly.

"'I don't wonder that you are surprised,' said she, and I could see that her fingers were trembling as she undid the fastenings of her mantle. 'Why, I never remember having done such a thing in my life before. The fact is that I felt as though I were choking and had a perfect longing for a breath of fresh air. I really think that I should have fainted if I had not gone out. I stood at the door for a few minutes, and now I am quite myself again.'

"All the time that she was telling me this story she never once looked in my direction, and her voice was quite unlike her usual tones. It was evident to me that she was saying what was false. I said nothing in reply, but turned my face to the wall, sick at heart, with my mind filled with a thousand venomous doubts and suspicions. What was it that my wife was concealing from me? Where had she been during that strange expedition? I felt that I should have no peace until I knew, and yet I shrank from asking her again after once she had told me what was false. All the rest of the night I tossed and tumbled, framing theory after theory, each more unlikely than the last.

"I should have gone to the City that day, but I was too disturbed in my mind to be able to pay attention to business matters. My wife seemed to be as upset as myself, and I could see from the little questioning glances which she kept shooting at me that she understood that I disbelieved her statement, and that she was at her wit's end what to do. We hardly exchanged a word during breakfast, and immediately afterwards I went out for a walk that I might think the matter out in the fresh morning air.

"I went as far as the Crystal Palace, spent an hour in the grounds, and was back in Norbury by one o'clock. It happened that my way took me past the cottage, and I stopped for an instant to look at the windows and to see if I could catch a glimpse of the strange face which had looked out at me on the day before. As I stood there, imagine my surprise, Mr Holmes, when the door suddenly opened and my wife walked out.

"I was struck dumb with astonishment at the sight of her, but my emotions were nothing to those which showed themselves upon her face when our eyes met. She seemed for an instant to wish to shrink back inside the house again; and then, seeing how useless all concealment must be, she came forward, with a very white face and frightened eyes which belied the smile upon her lips.

"'Ah, Jack,' she said, 'I have just been in to see if I can be of any assistance to our new neighbours. Why do you look at me like that, Jack? You are not angry with me?'

"'So,' said I, 'this is where you went during the night.'

"'What do you mean?' she cried.

"'You came here. I am sure of it. Who are these people that you should visit them at such an hour?'

"'I have not been here before.'

"'How can you tell me what you know is false?' I cried. 'Your very voice changes as you speak. When have I ever had a secret from you? I shall enter that cottage, and I shall probe the matter to the bottom.'

"'No, no, Jack, for God's sake!' she gasped in uncontrollable emotion. Then, as I approached the door, she seized my sleeve and pulled me back with convulsive strength.

"'I implore you not to do this, Jack,' she cried. 'I swear that I will tell you everything some day, but nothing but misery can come of it if you enter that cottage.' Then, as I tried to shake her off, she clung to me in a frenzy of entreaty.

"'Trust me, Jack!' she cried. 'Trust me only this once. You will never have cause to regret it. You know that I would not have a secret from you if it were not for your own sake. Our whole lives are at stake in this. If you come home with me all will be well. If you force your way into that cottage all is over between us.'

"There was such earnestness, such despair, in her manner that her words arrested me, and I stood irresolute before the door.

"'I will trust you on one condition, and on one condition only,' said I at last. 'It is that this mystery comes to an end from now. You are at liberty to preserve your secret, but you must promise me that there shall be no more nightly visits, no more doings which are kept from my knowledge. I am willing to forget those which are past if you will promise that there shall be no more in the future.'

"'I was sure that you would trust me,' she cried with a great sigh of relief. 'It shall be just as you wish. Come away—oh, come away up to the house.'

"Still pulling at my sleeve, she led me away from the cottage. As we went I glanced back, and there was that yellow livid face watching us out of the upper window. What link could there be between that creature and my wife? Or how could the coarse, rough woman whom I had seen the day before be connected with her? It was a strange puzzle, and yet I knew that my mind could never know ease again until I had solved it.

"For two days after this I stayed at home, and my wife appeared to abide loyally by our engagement, for, as far as I know, she never stirred out of the house. On the third day however, I had ample evidence that her solemn promise was not enough to hold her back from this secret influence which drew her away from her husband and her duty.

"I had gone into town on that day, but I returned by the 2:40 instead of the 3:36, which is my usual train. As I entered the house the maid ran into the hall with a startled face.

"'Where is your mistress?' I asked.

"'I think that she has gone out for a walk,' she answered.

"My mind was instantly filled with suspicion. I rushed upstairs to make sure that she was not in the house. As I did so I happened to glance out of one of the upper windows and saw the maid with whom I had just been speaking running across the field in the direction of the cottage. Then of course I saw exactly what it all meant. My wife had gone over there and had asked the servant to call her if I should return. Tingling with anger, I rushed down and hurried across, determined to end the matter once and forever. I saw my wife and the maid hurrying back along the lane, but I did not stop to speak with them. In the cottage lay the secret which was casting a shadow over my life. I vowed that, come what might, it should be a secret no longer. I did not even knock when I reached it, but turned the handle and rushed into the passage.

"It was all still and quiet upon the ground floor. In the kitchen a kettle was singing on the fire, and a large black cat lay coiled up in the basket; but there was no sign of the woman whom I had seen before. I ran into the other room, but it was equally deserted. Then I rushed up the stairs only to find two other rooms empty and deserted at the top. There was no one at all in the whole house. The furniture and pictures were of the most common and vulgar description, save in the one chamber at the window of which I had seen the strange face. That was comfortable and elegant, and all my suspicions rose into a fierce, bitter flame when I saw that on the mantelpiece stood a copy of a full-length photograph of my wife, which had been taken at my request only three months ago.

"I stayed long enough to make certain that the house was absolutely empty. Then I left it, feeling a weight at my heart such as I had never had before. My wife came out into the hall as I entered my house; but I was too hurt and angry to speak with her, and, pushing past her, I made my way into my study. She followed me, however, before I could close the door.

"'I am sorry that I broke my promise, Jack,' said she, 'but if you knew all the circumstances I am sure that you would forgive me.'

"'Tell me everything, then,' said I.

"'I cannot, Jack, I cannot,' she cried.

"'Until you tell me who it is that has been living in that cottage, and who it is to whom you have given that photograph, there can never be any confidence between us,' said I, and breaking away from her I left the house. That was yesterday, Mr Holmes, and I have not seen her since, nor do I know anything more about this strange business. It is the first shadow that has come between us, and it has so shaken me that I do not know what I should do for the best. Suddenly this morning it occurred to me that you were the man to advise me, so I have hurried to you now, and I place myself unreservedly in your hands. If there is any point which I have not made clear, pray question me about it. But, above all, tell me quickly what I am to do, for this misery is more than I can bear."

Holmes and I had listened with the utmost interest to this extraordinary statement, which had been delivered in the jerky, broken fashion of a man who is under the influence of extreme emotion. My companion sat silent now for some time, with his chin upon his hand, lost in thought.

"Tell me," said he at last, "could you swear that this was a man's face which you saw at the window?"

"Each time that I saw it I was some distance away from it so that it is impossible for me to say."

"You appear, however, to have been disagreeably impressed by it."

"It seemed to be of an unusual colour and to have a strange rigidity about the features. When I approached it vanished with a jerk."

"How long is it since your wife asked you for a hundred pounds?"

"Nearly two months."

"Have you ever seen a photograph of her first husband?"

"No, there was a great fire at Atlanta very shortly after his death, and all her papers were destroyed."

"And yet she had a certificate of death. You say that you saw it."

"Yes, she got a duplicate after the fire."

"Did you ever meet anyone who knew her in America?"

"No."

"Did she ever talk of revisiting the place?"

"No."

"Or get letters from it?

"No."

"Thank you. I should like to think over the matter a little now. If the cottage is now permanently deserted we may have some difficulty. If, on the other hand, as I fancy is more likely the inmates were warned of your coming and left before you entered yesterday, then they may be back now, and we should clear it all up easily. Let me advise you, then, to return to Norbury and to examine the windows of the cottage again. If you have reason to believe that it is inhabited, do not force your way in, but send a wire to my friend and me. We shall be with you within an hour of receiving it, and we shall then very soon get to the bottom of the business."

"And if it is still empty?"

"In that case I shall come out to-morrow and talk it over with you. Good-bye, and, above all, do not fret until you know that you really have a cause for it."

"I am afraid that this is a bad business, Watson," said my companion as he returned after accompanying Mr Grant Munro to the door. "What do you make of it?"

"It had an ugly sound," I answered.

"Yes. There's blackmail in it, or I am much mistaken."

"And who is the blackmailer?"

"Well, it must be the creature who lives in the only comfortable room in the place and has her photograph above his fireplace. Upon my word, Watson, there is something very attractive about that livid face at the window, and I would not have missed the case for worlds."

"You have a theory?"

"Yes, a provisional one. But I shall be surprised if it does not turn out to be correct. This woman's first husband is in that cottage."

"Why do you think so?"

"How else can we explain her frenzied anxiety that her second one should not enter it? The facts, as I read them, are something like this: This woman was married in America. Her husband developed some hateful qualities, or shall we say he contracted some loathsome disease and became a leper or an imbecile? She flies from him at last, returns to England, changes her name, and starts her life, as she thinks, afresh. She has been married three years and believes that her position is quite secure, having shown her husband the death certificate of some man whose name she has assumed, when suddenly her whereabouts is discovered by her first husband, or, we may suppose, by some unscrupulous woman who has attached herself to the invalid. They write to the wife and threaten to come and expose her. She asks for a hundred pounds and endeavours to buy them off. They come in spite of it, and when the husband mentions casually to the wife that there are new-comers in the cottage, she knows in some way that they are her pursuers. She waits until her husband is asleep and then she rushes down to endeavour to persuade them to leave her in peace. Having no success, she goes again next morning, and her husband meets her, as he has told us, as she comes out. She promises him then not to go there again, but two days afterwards the hope of getting rid of those dreadful neighbours was too strong for her, and she made another attempt, taking down with her the photograph which had probably been demanded from her. In the midst of this interview the maid rushed in to say that the master had come home, on which the wife, knowing that he would come straight down to the cot-tage, hurried the inmates out at the back door, into the grove of fir-trees, probably, which was mentioned as standing near. In this way he found the place deserted. I shall be very much surprised, however, if it is still so when he reconnoitres it this evening. What do you think of my theory?"

"It is all surmise."

But at least it covers all the facts. When new facts come to our knowledge which cannot be covered by it, it will be time enough to reconsider it. We can do nothing more until we have a message from our friend at Norbury."

But we had not a very long time to wait for that. It came just as we had finished our tea.

"The cottage is still tenanted. Have seen the face again at the window. Will meet the seven-o'clock train and will take no steps until you arrive."

He was waiting on the platform when we stepped out, and we could see in the light of the station lamps that he was very pale, and quivering with agitation.

"They are still there, Mr Holmes," said he, laying his hand hard upon my friend's sleeve. "I saw lights in the cottage as I came down. We shall settle it now once and for all."

"What is your plan, then?" asked Holmes as he walked down the dark tree-lined road.

"I am going to force my way in and see for myself who is in the house. I wish you both to be there as witnesses."

"You are quite determined to do this in spite of your wife's warning that it is better that you should not solve the mystery?"

"Yes, I am determined."

"Well, I think that you are in the right. Any truth is better than indefinite doubt. We had better go up at once. Of course, legally, we are putting ourselves hopelessly in the wrong; but I think that it is worth it."

It was a very dark night, and a thin rain began to fall as we turned from the highroad into a narrow lane, deeply rutted, with hedges on either side. Mr Grant Munro pushed impatiently forward, however, and we stumbled after him as best we could.

"There are the lights of my house," he murmured, pointing to a glimmer among the trees. "And here is the cottage which I am going to enter."

We turned a corner in the lane as he spoke, and there was the building close beside us. A yellow bar falling across the black foreground showed that the door was not quite closed, and one window in the upper story was brightly illuminated. As we looked, we saw a dark blur moving across the blind.

"There is that creature!" cried Grant Munro. "You can see for yourselves that someone is there. Now follow me, and we shall soon know all."

We approached the door, but suddenly a woman appeared out of the shadow and stood in the golden track of the lamplight. I could not see her face in the darkness, but her arms were thrown out in an attitude of entreaty.

"For God's sake, don't, Jack!" she cried. "I had a presentiment that you would come this evening. Think better of it, dear! Trust me again, and you will never have cause to regret it."

"I have trusted you too long, Effie," he cried sternly. "Leave go of me! I must pass you. My friends and I are going to settle this matter once and forever!" He pushed her to one side, and we followed closely after him. As he threw the door open an old woman ran out in front of him and tried to bar his passage, but he thrust her back, and an instant afterwards we were all upon the stairs. Grant Munro rushed into the lighted room at the top, and we entered at his heels.

It was a cosy, well-furnished apartment, with two candles burning upon the table and two upon the mantelpiece. In the corner, stooping over a desk, there sat what appeared to be a little girl. Her face was turned away as we entered, but we could see that she was dressed in a red frock, and that she had long white gloves on. As she whisked round to us, I gave a cry of surprise and horror. The face which she turned towards us was of the strangest livid tint, and the features were absolutely devoid of any expression. An instant later the mystery was explained. Holmes, with a laugh, passed his hand behind the child's ear, a mask peeled off from her countenance, and there was a little coal-black negress, with all her white teeth flashing in amusement at our amazed faces. I burst out laughing, out of sympathy with her merriment; but Grant Munro stood staring, with his hand clutching his throat.

"My God!" he cried. "What can be the meaning of this?"

"I will tell you the meaning of it," cried the lady, sweeping into the room with a proud, set face. "You have forced me, against my own judgment, to tell you, and now we must both make the best of it. My husband died at Atlanta. My child survived."

"Your child?"

She drew a large silver locket from her bosom. "You have never seen this open."

"I understood that it did not open."

She touched a spring, and the front hinged back. There was a portrait within of a man strikingly handsome and intelligent-looking, but bearing unmistakable signs upon his features of his African descent.

"That is John Hebron, of Atlanta," said the lady, "and a nobler man never walked the earth. I cut myself off from my race in order to wed him, but never once while he lived did I for an instant regret it. It was our misfortune that our only child took after his people rather than mine. It is often so in such matches, and little Lucy is darker far than ever her father was. But dark or fair, she is my own dear little girlie, and her mother's pet." The little creature ran across at the words and nestled up against the lady's dress. "When I left her in America," she continued, "it was only because her health was weak, and the change might have done her harm. She was given to the care of a faithful Scotch woman who had once been our servant. Never for an instant did I dream of disowning her as my child. But when chance threw you in my way, Jack, and I learned to love you, I feared to tell you about my child. God forgive me, I feared that I should lose you, and I had not the courage to tell you. I had to choose between you, and in my weakness I turned away from my own little girl. For three years I have kept her existence a secret from you, but I heard from the nurse, and I knew that all was well with her. At last, however, there came an overwhelming desire to see the child once more. I struggled against it, but in vain. Though I knew the danger, I determined to have the child over, if it were but for a few weeks. I sent a hundred pounds to the nurse, and I gave her instructions about this cottage, so that she might come as a neighbour, without my appearing to be in any way connected with her. I pushed my precautions so far as to order her to keep the child in the house during the daytime, and to cover up her little face and hands so that even those who might see her at the window should not gossip about there being a black child in the neighbourhood. If I had been less cautious I might have been more wise, but I was half crazy with fear that you should learn the truth.

"It was you who told me first that the cottage was occupied. I should have waited for the morning, but I could not sleep for excitement, and so at last I slipped out, knowing how difficult it is to awake you. But you saw me go, and that was the beginning of my troubles. Next day you had my secret at your mercy, but you nobly refrained from pursuing your advantage. Three days later, however, the nurse and child only just escaped from the back door as you rushed in at the front one. And now to-night you at last know all, and I ask you what is to become of us, my child and me?" She clasped her hands and waited for an answer.

It was a long two minutes before Grant Munro broke the silence, and when his answer came it was one of which I love to think. He lifted the little child, kissed her, and then, still carrying her, he held his other hand out to his wife and turned towards the door.

"We can talk it over more comfortably at home," said he. "I am not a very good man, Effie, but I think that I am a better one than you have given me credit for being."

Holmes and I followed them down the lane, and my friend plucked at my sleeve as we came out.

"I think," said he, "that we shall be of more use in London than in Norbury."

Not another word did he say of the case until late that night, when he was turning away, with his lighted candle, for his bedroom.

"Watson," said he, "if it should ever strike you that I am getting a little overconfident in my powers, or giving less pains to a case than it deserves, kindly whisper 'Norbury' in my ear, and I shall be infinitely obliged to you."